TOM GALLACHER

Tom Gallacher was best known as a playwright until
the publication of APPRENTICE which won a 1983
Scottish Arts Council award. His greatest achieve-
ments in the theatre were the three plays, MR JOYCE
IS LEAVING PARIS, SCHELLENBRACK and RE-
VIVAL! Apart from London, Tom Gallacher has worked in Denmark, Germany, New York, Edinburgh and
Dublin. Now returned to Scotland and living in Glasgow, he has turned to writing fiction full-time.

Tom Gallacher's previous book JOURNEYMAN, is
also published in Sceptre. His collection of short
stories, THE JEWEL MAKER, also won a Scottish
Arts Council award. Tom Gallacher's most recent
novel is THE WIND ON THE HEATH.

Tom Gallacher

APPRENTICE

British Library C.I.P.

Gallacher, Tom
  Apprentice.
  I. Title
  823'.914[F]   PR6057.A388

  ISBN 0-340-42145-2

Printed and bound in Great Britain
for Hodder and Stoughton Paper-
backs, a division of Hodder and
Stoughton Limited, Mill Road, Dun-
ton Green, Sevenoaks, Kent TN13
2YA (Editorial Office: 47 Bedford
Square, London WC1B 3DP) by
Richard Clay Limited, Bungay,
Suffolk. Photoset by Rowland
Phototypesetting Limited, Bury St
Edmunds, Suffolk.

CONTENTS

Preface

It was the shipyard labourer, a man known to all as Lord Sweatrag, who advised me to keep a notebook which would record my progress to becoming a marine engineer. In the event, I found it did nothing of the kind. Instead of the Strength of Materials, the Theory of Machines, the Calculus and Steam Entropy, the notebook is full of people. Five years serving my time serves instead those spirited, funny, maddening people to whom I was an outsider. They criss-cross and collide through every entry; appearing, dis-appearing, re-appearing – governed by reasons which were rarely apparent to me. And that, probably, is how they should be presented – as a continuous roll of inter-mingled lives. But I was a young man when I made the notes, and therefore possessed of the fallacy that these vivid, individual people somehow existed only for my benefit. So what was true of them outside my personal intervention and knowledge is missing. Unfortunately, I do not have the ability to invent it. That being the case, it seemed that the best thing to do was *un*wind the intermingling threads and present the people in separate stories; one for each year of my apprenticeship.

Even so, there are some characters who insist on intruding at times and in circumstances where the matter does not concern them. I've let them do it because I could not, for example, deny them the use of public transport or access to the pubs, the river, or the grimy precipitous streets of Greenock in the 1950s; particularly since I've kept them waiting for close on thirty years. The delay is due to a fundamental mistake of mine. I thought that having qualified as an engineer it followed that my life should be devoted to engineering. Until recently that is how, and why, I have wasted my time. But I kept the notebooks safe, cherishing the delusion that some day I'd try to make proper use of them. I was over forty before that day arrived. It was at a funeral and I decided I would quit engineering altogether. I don't know why it took me so long to realise that, when I was in Greenock, it was not my true function to be an apprentice engineer but an apprentice human being. My teachers were the people in this book. I wish they'd had more success.

W. T.

Portrait of Isa Mulvenny

For me, the Past begins at Euston. That is, Euston in the mid-Fifties at about ten o'clock in the evening. In summer months it was still clear enough to sit out in that little front garden with a good view of the splendid archway which, eventually, could not be saved. Winter and summer I arrived in plenty of time for the journey back to my apprenticeship on the Clyde after Fair holidays, Christmas holidays and at the end of strikes. Each time I walked under that arch I felt a little less English than the time before; each time more convinced that my separate Scottish identity was the real one. They should have a Customs Post at Euston.

Now – again – I am going down the ramp to that interminable platform which curves out into the dark. The train is in place and already crowded with people who will keep their vigil sitting up all night, confronting each other with stoic resentment. In the past I did that, but now I walk on, beyond their carriages, and they glance at me as though a threat has passed. Somewhere, if I can find it, my name is posted on a window as a first-class sleeper to Glasgow. I wish I could believe it.

'Good evening, sir,' says the sleeping-car attendant, genially hovering at the door.

'Thompson.'

'Aye, Mr Thompson. That's er . . . number eleven. Is that all the luggage ye've got?'

'Yes. I'll be coming back tomorrow.'

He effaces himself in a corner to allow me to squeeze past him and move down the corridor. But apparently he is still short of information. 'Jist a wee business trip, eh?'

11

'No.'

'Ah, well . . . there you are, sir. Number eleven. I'll take your ticket the now and no' disturb ye later.' I take off my raincoat to get at the ticket, and thereby give him another clue. 'Oh, I didnae notice the uniform outside there. Merchant Navy, eh? Engineer?'

'That's right. Here you are.'

The train starts. 'Thank you, sir. That's us off now. You're jist in time, Mr Thompson.'

'I hope so. Good night.'

'Er . . . will you wish tea in the mornin'?'

'Yes, please. About half an hour before we get in.'

'Certainly, sir. Good night. Sleep tight.'

That's what Isa said. I heard her voice echo it as she, smiling, withdrew from the room. 'Good night, sleep tight, don't let the bugs bite. If they bite, squeeze them tight. Well . . . ' she shrugged with great good humour, 'there's no' much else ye can dae wi' bugs, is there?' She laughed heartily and closed the door. That was the first night I slept at the Mulvennys'. Isa's new lodger, aged sixteen. I thought she was joking about the bed-bugs and what to do with them. But she wasn't. In the morning I complained to her about the marks they left on me. 'Tut, tut, tut. You must have a very sensitive skin, son.' I thought that, on the other hand, it could be she bred ferocious bugs. 'But don't you worry, son. I'll get rid of them.' Very sympathetic, Isa. Made me wish I hadn't mentioned it. Maybe I could get used to being covered in angry red blotches – like all her previous lodgers; probably. However, Isa did know an antidote. When I came back from my first day at the shipyard, she was out on the stairhead landing.

She was on her knees, hammer in hand, smashing camphor balls. She peered down through the cast-iron railings when she heard my feet on the stair. 'Is that you back already? Your tea'll no' be long.'

'What are you doing, Mrs Mulvenny?'

'Camphor . . . ' Smash. 'Best thing for bugs.' Smash. 'But ye cannae lie on lumps of it, so I have tae . . . ' – smash – ' . . . crush the stuff. Feel it. Quite fine powder that, eh?'

I rubbed some of the violent smelling powder between my fingers. 'Yes, it is. But can't you buy it as a powder?'

'I don't think so. Anyway, I always get the balls and smash them. And it's better out here on the landing where there's a stone floor. D'ye think that'll be enough?'

'Yes, I should think so. Do you just sprinkle it on the bed?'

She laughed. 'Oh, no! Under the sheet. You'll hardly notice it. Except for the smell.' She gathered the sheets of newspaper together, making a pile of the white crystalline powder. 'There. I'll let you by. Young Andy's in, and ma man should be back shortly. Watch yer feet! I'll clean that mess the morra. It's my turn for the stairs.'

She followed me into the dark lobby which was much restricted by the huge coal-box behind the front door. An ornate sideboard ran the full length of the other wall. She called to her schoolboy son. 'Andy! Here's Bill now.' A dark-haired, truculent youth emerged from the kitchen.

'You got a start in the yard,' he said.

'Yes, I started today.'

'My father's a charge-hand there. In the plate shop.'

'Oh.'

My limited response must have meant that I did not understand the significance of this, so he went on, 'That's like a foreman . . . ye know. One of the gaffers. What's your father do?'

'He's an engineer.'

'At a desk or at the tools?' he challenged me. From the front room, where she was dealing death to the bugs in my bed, came the sound – and the very sweet sound – of Isa singing 'The Rose of Tralee'.

'He's a consultant,' I said.

'Huh. That's like a Doctor.'

'He's a doctor of Science.'

'And he's put you in a shipyard!' There was an even mixture of scorn and disbelief in his voice, so that I could take either – depending on whether or not I was lying about this odd arrangement.

'*He* started in a shipyard,' I explained.

Andy swivelled slightly, so that his back rested flat and

13

easy against the wall. 'I'm studying to be an accountant,' he said.

'Oh.' The subject did not interest me. I had but one pressing idea in mind. 'Could I wash before we eat?' It seemed that now would be the time when I'd discover where the bathroom was. The previous night I had been shown the lavatory on the half-landing of the outer stair, but no bathroom.

Andy called to his mother, who was now in the kitchen. 'Ma! He wants to wash!'

She called back. 'Certainly. I'll let him in here at the sink as soon as I've strained these potatoes.'

There was no bathroom. And Andy was not yet finished with my briefing. 'My father's a runner. Cross country. That's all his medals and cups and plaques there on the sideboard.'

'Really.' I was tired of standing, oily-handed, in the lobby.

'He won them. Does your father go in for any sport?'

'No. He's, er . . . too fat.'

Andy had clearly gained the advantage at last. He smiled and went on in a much more pleasant tone, 'Ma Da' won all them. Outright. Wi' the Harriers, mainly. This year he's sure tae get the Levi-Allen Shield.'

Isa clashed a pot lid in place and called to me, 'There you are, Billy. In you get and give yer hands a rub.'

The table was set in the kitchen for the evening meal. Isa had cleared a place for me at the sink which was banked with pots and pans, with piles of vegetable peelings stacked neatly in the corners. As I tucked my elbows close to my sides and sluiced my hands under the tap, I remarked to her, 'Mr Mulvenny has won a lot of trophies.'

'What, son?'

'I was admiring the trophies.'

'He means the silver,' shouted Andy from the lobby. The Mulvennys preferred calling to each other from separate rooms rather than conversing in the same room.

'Aw, aye! The silver.' Isa accepted the translation without looking up. 'Next week he runs in the Leafy Allan. We'll put that in the middle.'

'If he wins.'

Isa tucked her chin and gave me a tolerant glance. 'He'll win all right. Nae fear aboot that. There's nobody can touch Andrew at the runnin'.' We heard the front door open then slam shut. 'That'll be him noo.'

'Hello, Da,' Andy greeted his father.

'Andy,' observed Mr Mulvenny's voice, completing the ritual. He was a man who expected to be met, however laconically, and Andy was certainly the person he expected to meet him.

'I'm in here, Andrew,' called Mrs Mulvenny.

'Where the hell else would ye be?' her husband shouted back.

Isa laughed, delightedly. 'Aye! Where else, indeed!'

Mr Mulvenny appeared in the kitchen doorway and everything about him defied even the suspicion that he had just returned from the grimy plate-shop of a shipyard. 'Well, how's our new apprentice?' he asked me.

'Jist gettin' ready to eat,' Isa told him.

'It wasn't too bad,' I admitted.

'Dirty work, though.'

'Yes.'

Mr Mulvenny sucked a deep breath through his teeth and drily smacked his lips at the end of it. 'Well, them that can't do better have to show the signs o' it. And I've done my share, eh. But I'm grateful my son'll never have to get his hands dirty.'

'It washes off,' I said.

'Sure. At first. After a while, though, nothing'll shift it. Aye. Them that can't do better have to show the signs o' it.' He took off his jacket, and folded it over the back of his chair. When he sat at the table he sat with a perfectly straight, unsupported spine.

'That's your place, Billy,' said Isa, hovering, pot in hand. 'Sit there.' Young Andy was already seated and I realised, with surprise, that the table was set for only three people. Mrs Mulvenny stayed on her feet, tending and serving, until we were finished. This was necessary, apparently, because they did not use serving dishes on the table. The food was served straight from the pots, kept warm and in need of stirring, on the stove. Only when Mr Mulvenny was settled with his evening paper at the fire and Andy had gone to his bedroom would Mrs Mulvenny sit down to eat. We had almost finished our meal when Mr Mulvenny spoke to his wife again. 'Did you tell him about the room?'

She was immediately contrite. 'Oooh! I did not.'

'Isa!' his voice grated with instant irritation.

'I would have remembered, though. Before next week.' Then, less sure, 'I expect.'

Switching on his reasonable tone, Andrew turned to me. 'Well, you see, Bobby . . .'

' "Billy",' his wife corrected.

'Billy. You've got the front room and that's where we have . . .'

Isa babbled, unsuppressed, 'Because the piana's there and wi' the . . .'

'Isa!' She stopped. He continued. 'Because it's the biggest room, we have our wee celebrations there. I don't suppose . . .'

'You'll enjoy yourself.'

' . . . you'll mind. They never go on very late. You'll be able to join in the sing-song.'

'When?' I asked.

Andrew smiled modestly. 'Well, whenever I win another lump o' silver. Just a few neighbours, ye know. And friends.' Clearly, these were separate groups.

'Joe Harper's a great man on the keyboard and Isa gives us a song.'

'The same song,' said Andy.

'Well, they like it,' retorted his mother.

'They've nae choice,' said Andrew. 'And she usually manages tae break a few dishes into the bargain.'

'I do not!'

'Of course, there have been times when things got a bit rowdy. I remember one time . . . now, when was it? The Western Division Challenge Cup, I think it was . . .'

'That's right,' confirmed Andy.

'When I won that for the third time. A field of over a hundred, mind you . . . and some well-trained opposition.'

Whatever the opposition Andrew had to face running

across fields, he never had to face any opposition at home. And, of course, he won the Levi-Allen Shield – outright. It joined the Western Division Challenge Cup on the gleaming altar of silver piled along the lobby sideboard.

Meanwhile, I had to get used to conditions at work and to learn as quickly as possible the shop-floor hierarchy. To begin with I was preoccupied in getting used to the sheer height and length of those glass-roofed, aircraft-hangar spaces which are so cosily called 'shops'; the row on row of different machines set into the concrete floor and each provided with its wood-spar footboard; the 'clear' alleys inviolately defined by fresh painted lines; the piles of metal and neat stacks of finished pieces; and straddling all this, overhead, the heavy cranes patrolling to and fro, controlled by unseen drivers who themselves could see the smallest gesture which might summon them. Compared with all that, the men were insignificant and identical, except that the foreman wore a suit – and a soft hat which, apparently, he never removed in public. He ruled his department from a little wooden hut. It was like a small garden shed set indoors, leaning against the soaring whitewashed wall which rose sixty or seventy feet to the glass roof.

Immediately outside 'the box' was a long trestle table in front of a bank of filing cabinets. That was the domain of the foreman's chief assistant, the charge-hand. He was responsible for all the working drawings that came to the department. The charge-hand had no real power but was an invaluable intermediary and was a great retailer of information in both directions. Then there were senior journeymen who all wore caps and junior journeymen who rarely did until they were thirty, or were blessed with premature baldness. Then came the apprentices in strict order of their year, from fifth to first. Last were the servants of all these – the labourers. I never discovered if they had their own pecking-order because if there was anything that the youngest apprentice wanted done, even the oldest labourer would have to do it.

Frank Fogel and I were the youngest apprentices that week in March, 1955. We had our medical together and received our Works Number together. Frank was 874, I was

875. These numbers were die-stamped on brass discs called 'tickets' and were used as a check of our arrival and departure from work by the Gatehouse keeper and also our bowel movements in the works lavatories by the Shithouse keeper. The urinals could be used without handing over the 'ticket'.

Frank explained. 'That's because a piss takes less than three minutes an' ye don't sit doon for it.' He gave me a suspicious glance. 'At least, *A* don't.'

'Do you think we have to memorise the number?' I asked him.

'Not at all!' he scoffed. 'Jist get it branded on yer arm, there. The important thing is, *they* don't hiv tae remember yer name.' He laughed. 'An' I know ye've memorised that.'

I wished that I felt as self-assured as he sounded. Of course, he'd already worked for a year outside. While waiting for his sixteenth birthday he'd taken a job as a van-boy with a bakery roundsman. I was grateful that he seemed disposed to be my general guide; also, my interpreter of the foreign language spoken in that part of Scotland. His first words to me were, 'Siv us a li', i' ye fulla?' which turned out to mean, 'Would you give me a light?'. Even in that first week he started the habit of adding a translation to anything he said which, by my expression, he saw I had not understood. He was bilingual and understood everything I said, though my accent seemed to him fanciful.

'A hiv'tae laugh at the English,' he said. 'They wull miss oot the R's when there is an R, but when there *isnae* wan they put it in.'

'Do we?'

'Aye!' To illustrate the point he invited me, 'Say, "the warmest girl in the world".' I did so and he pointed victoriously at my mouth. 'D'ye see whi' A mean? Noo say, "Law and Order".' Again I complied and, delighted at my manifest failure with the R, he delivered the whole damning sentence in my voice, ' "The wa'mist gel in the w'old is Lauren Auda." A'm tellin' ye – if ye wrote doon English as *you* speak, it wid look ridiculous.'

For the party, my bed, still smelling richly of camphor,

was disguised as a divan and Isa, gawky and exuberant, prepared to entertain. Her long, beautiful hair was elaborately braided and coiled. Since it was a special occasion, she wore make-up. The effect betrayed lack of practice. She also wore her 'costume'. That is, a matching jacket and skirt; a tailored suit, in fact. She thought it made her look 'not so tall'. But really it did nothing for her height and only added to the impression that she was a gate-crasher at this assembly; an enthusiastic guest who'd escaped from a seedy wedding-reception somewhere else.

On this and many similar occasions, Mr Mulvenny held court, dressed in a neat dark suit, glowing with health and obvious fitness. His button-bright eyes darted in and out of the conversation, finding every lull that could be stretched to accommodate reference to his sporting achievement. His guests, aware of who was providing the drink, were apt at wrenching any subject instantly off-course to ensure that the object would be Andrew.

Isa was very proud of him. So was Andy. Usually, I was more preoccupied in praying that everyone would just go away and let me get to bed. That never happened until they had all done a 'turn', which usually involved singing. Joe Harper, a spry, prematurely old-looking man, was glued to the piano stool. Though undoubtedly 'shachly' – as they said in those parts – he had the jaunty assurance of a relentless entertainer. Perfectly willing as he was to accompany others, he had his own repertoire to get through. One item was always 'South of the Border':

'South of the border, I rode back one day,
There in a veil of white, by candlelight, she knelt to pray,
The Mission Bells told me that I must not stay,
South of the border, down Mexico way . . . '

Then we all joined in, 'Ay, Ay, Ay, Ay . . . ' Big finish, 'Ay, Ay, Ay, Ay-ya-yay!' And everyone applauded.

'Lovely, Joe,' said Andrew. 'Very nice indeed.'

But Isa went on singing, unaccompanied. ' . . . I lied as I whispered, "Mañana" – for our tomorrow never came. South of the . . . '

'We've finished it, Isa!' her husband shouted, and we all laughed.

She stopped singing, but added, 'I think it's very sad, that.'

'What?' asked Joe.

' "Mañana".'

'Eh?'

'Forget it, Isa,' her husband instructed. 'Fill up Joe's glass. It's thirsty work playin' the piana.'

The pianist eagerly agreed. 'It is that! Especially down Mexico way.' He accepted the refilled glass. 'Aw, ye're a good lassie, Isa.'

Joe's wife, Ella, a plump, tightly-bunched little woman, now turned to me. 'What's your name again, son?'

'Bill Thompson.'

'That's right. Well, it's time you did your turn.'

'I can't sing!'

'Even so, you'll have tae dae somethin' tae oblige the company.'

'Thank you, I'd rather not.'

She drew back, affronted, and mimicked my accent. 'Oh, really!' Then, overwhelmed by the insult, called to her husband, 'D'ye hear that, Joe?'

'Whiss-a'?'

'The boy here doesnae think much o' the entertainment.'

He swivelled round on the piano stool and squinted at me in a mock-humorous way through his cigarette smoke. 'Aw, that's a peety. We do our best.'

This seemed to me grossly unfair and I protested, 'No! I didn't say that.'

Isa, on the other side of the room, must have heard the concern in my raised voice and hurried over. 'What is it?'

But Ella was not willing to have the matter smoothed out by Isa just yet. 'Andrew!' she called. 'You'll hiv tae watch yer step as well, now ye've got such a choosey ludger.'

'I really didn't mean to . . .'

'Listen tae 'im!' cried Ella. It was my accent which annoyed her much more than my refusal to perform.

'What is the matter, Billy?' Isa asked me, very softly.

'I just said that I can't sing.'

'Never mind. Maybe ye can do a wee recitation.'

Blessedly, this possibility was interrupted by Joe who was concerned that attention had been too long off the champion. 'Andrew, I've meant tae ask you . . .'

'What's that, Joe?'

'Are there any exercises I could do tae . . . Oh, I know I could never be as fit as you, but I'd like to . . .'

'I know what you mean.' He sprang up, prepared to demonstrate. 'Well, here's one. See how my feet are placed. Then ye just . . .'

His wife, who knew exactly what was coming next, felt she could afford to pursue her suggestion to me. 'Jist a wee recitation, that ye learned at school, maybe.'

'I don't know if I can remember anything.'

Ella sighed noisily. 'Ahhh, leave him alane, Isa. It disnae bother me. It's jist I never expected tae meet a stuck-up youngster in *your* hoose.' This meant that, now, Isa was somewhat to blame. Then attention was switched again to the acrobatic Andrew as he completed his very stylish exercise.

Joe was stunned. 'Och, I could never do that!'

'All it needs is a bit o' practice. See! Here's another wan.'

Ella halted him in mid-swing. 'I'd think you might have somethin' tae say about that, Andrew.'

'What? About what?'

'Just watchin' you gives me an awful drouth,' said Joe, unwilling to abandon, or prolong, his preparatory work.

The good hostess took over. 'Hand me yer glass.'

'You're the girl for me, Isa. Ooops!' She fumbled the changeover and the glass smashed on the edge of the piano stool. She flicked the fragments under the stool and got another.

'Stuck-up youngsters,' muttered the tenacious Ella.

'He's remembered something,' said Isa, pouring for Joe. 'Haven't ye, son?'

'Yes, I think so.'

'That's the boy.'

'Order! Order!' cried the pianist and played a portentous chord.

' "Abou Ben Adam",' I announced and began:

'Abou Ben Adam, may his tribe increase,
Awoke one night from a deep dream of peace,
And saw . . .
And saw in the moonlight of his room,
Making it rich like a lily in bloom –
An angel, writing in a book of gold . . .'

I paused. The next line refused to drop into my memory. Mentally I did a quick re-run of the opening, racing up to the blockage as though I might hurdle it with sheer speed. That didn't work and I repeated aloud, ' " . . . rich . . . like a lily in bloom . . . An angel . . ." '

'Another angel,' hissed Ella sceptically.

'Shhh!' cautioned Isa. But silence was no help. I was finished.

'That's a very short poem,' my tormentor observed.

'But very nice,' said Isa, leading a round of applause that nobody followed. 'And now it's time tae do my turn. Joe?' He at once launched into a florid introduction to 'The Rose of Tralee'.

'What's that tune called?' Andrew, heavily waggish, asked of the company.

'Och, you!' She aimed a playful swipe at him and he leapt nimbly away. Then she sang. She sang quite beautifully. Her sweet, light voice was transportingly clear and confident. But she seemed surprised, as surprised as anyone hearing her for the first time that she possessed so obviously fine a talent. There she stood, ungainly at the piano, badly made-up, the willing butt of so many jokes – singing with a pure spirit that held all of us enthralled. Even Andrew, I noticed, was gazing raptly towards her. And on that instant I knew intuitively why she always sang that song. It was his favourite. She sang for him. And he was affected by it. Indeed, *only* when she sang could one detect any outward sign of Mr Mulvenny's fondness for his wife. His habitual expression to her of impatient condescension changed to that of wonder. And while such moments lasted, both of them looked curiously young and vulnerable.

Apart from celebrating his victories, it was our duty to watch Andrew achieving them. Since he was a cross-country runner, this always had to be done at a distance and, apparently, through heavy rain. Sometimes – when there was a roadway close to the route – Mrs Mulvenny was an observer, but usually it was Andy and I who trudged from one vantage point to another then waited for the straggling line of runners to go piston-squelching past. Most of them looked as though they'd rather be doing *anything* else rather than what they were doing. Andrew, though, looked as though he was enjoying it. He also managed to look *cleaner* than any of the others when, as was usually the case, he came in first. And there, waiting for him on a bare little trestle-table, was the latest trophy. He was the only athlete I'd ever seen bow when he was given the prize. And whatever it was – cup or shield or plaque – when his name had been added to it, he would hand the prize to Mrs Mulvenny when he got home. It was *she* who'd place it on the lobby sideboard. To my relief, it was only for genuine silver trophies that parties were held.

Even so, my undisputed right to sole possession of the front room was steadily eroded. Andrew just could not imagine that anyone, other than himself, had a right to privacy. Often when I came back in the evening or on a week-end afternoon I'd find him there. Evidently he could see nothing wrong in that, but it annoyed me a great deal.

'Were you looking for something, Mr Mulvenny?'

'What's that, Billy!?' He turned in a leisurely fashion from the window.

'I wondered if you were looking for something.'

'No. I was just looking across the park, there. They're thinkin' of buildin' a sports centre, I believe.'

'Are they?'

He nodded and gave his attention once more to the wide and overgrown field which stretched from the back fence to steep rise of the hill. 'It's time they had some facilities in this area,' he said.

'Mr Mulvenny, did you have any lodgers before me?'

'No. Why'd you ask?'

'Because it seems you can't get used to the idea that this is my room.'

I had all his attention now. He crinkled his eyes. '*Your* room?'

'Yes.' For such a small man he was very intimidating but I'd made up my mind that this was something which had to be cleared up. 'While I am paying you rent it is my room.'

'So? Who says it's not?'

'Well . . . you seem to use it quite a lot.'

'The parties, you mean? Now, Billy, we explained at the outset that . . .'

'No. I don't mean the . . .'

'Don't you interrupt me!' He started rocking to and fro on the balls of his feet and his eyes glittered.

'I'm sorry.'

'It'll get ye nowhere comin' the high and mighty here, m'boy. We explained about the parties the first night you were here and you agreed it would be all right.'

I allowed a couple of beats of silence before I replied, 'Yes. That is all right. I didn't mean the parties.'

'When dae A use it any other time?'

'You are often in here. Like you are here now.'

He gasped with incredulity. 'Is that what you call "using" your room?'

'Aren't you?'

'I was lookin' out the window. I walked into an empty room and looked out the window. How does that interfere wi' you? Don't be daft.' He shook his head and padded away from me. 'Hah! Ye'll be wantin' a lock on the door next.'

'Yes. I do want a lock on the door.'

He came swinging back to poise himself directly in front of me and almost hissed, 'Well, you can want all you like, boy, but I'll have no locks on the doors inside my own house.' The full force of such a bizarre request struck him. 'What a cheek!'

'It's quite usual, Mr Mulvenny.'

'It's no' usual for me.'

'I'm sure if you had another lodger, he'd expect the same.'

'There won't be another. There wouldn't be you if it wasnae for young Andy.'

'What?'

'You were supposed tae have *his* room – when he went tae college.'

'But he still had a year at school when I arrived.'

'Aye, well. That's because he had tae repeat his last year at school to get the certificate for the college.'

'I see.'

'Oh, he got it all right. Be startin' at the Accountancy College in the Autumn. That'll mean *he* has tae go into digs in Glasgow – so, *your* money was tae pay for that.' He gave me a sharp admonitory nod. 'Ye can be sure it's only for his sake I'd put up wi' a lodger.'

'In that case, could I make a suggestion?'

'Okay. What is it?'

'When Andy's looking at digs, could you tell him to make sure there's a lock on the door.'

Andrew gave the slightest grimace of discomfiture. 'I'll tell him,' he said. 'And maybe, in the Autumn, you could move intae the wee room.'

'No. I'm sorry, I won't.'

'In that case, Billy, you'd better put up wi' things the way they are – or get out altogether.' I thought he would leave me to think about it but he wanted an answer there and then. 'Fair enough?' he prodded, waiting for surrender.

'I'll stay.'

At the door he gave me a tight little smile. 'I thought ye would.'

The moment he'd gone I discovered that I was holding myself tense and feeling suddenly tired. Other people, too, remarked that Andrew had a draining effect upon them. He seemed so packed with controlled energy. It was as though any antagonism to him induced a dangerously high voltage and if you stood close enough you became either a fuse wire or an earthing device. At seventeen, I was a rather thin fuse wire. After that interview my integrity was blown as far as Mr Mulvenny was concerned. For me it seemed enough that, whereas I hadn't won my point, I had at least made my point. Less reassuring was the discovery that I amounted to no more than away-from-home expenses for Andy.

In the year I'd spent at the Mulvennys I had noted the faith that Andrew had in his son but could find no possible justification for it. And perhaps it was because Andy himself had difficulty finding justification for it that he tried so hard to please his father in matters where neither intelligence nor ability were required.

One afternoon, when we were out to watch a race that never reached us, we were caught in a downpour that couldn't be ignored and took shelter in a linesman's hut by the railway. 'Why do we do this?' I wondered aloud as I peered out at the water bouncing off the sleepers.

'A don't know why *you* do it,' said Andy, with unusual candour.

'Doesn't he expect us to?'

'He expects me tae watch 'im.'

'But you're interested in running, aren't you?'

'No' in the least! But my faither thinks A am.'

We were, necessarily, standing very close together. That, the heady smell of creosote, the confessional-box dimensions of the hut and an utterly miserable and wasted afternoon had apparently broken down Andy's normally defensive attitude. I couldn't let the opportunity slip, but started lightly enough. 'Maybe that's because you tell him you're interested. And you remember where and when he won everything he's ever won.'

'A don't remember them. A memorise them. It's jist a matter o' studyin' all thae trophies on the lobby table.'

I was amazed. 'Do you?'

He nodded sadly. 'Oh, aye. That an' the club records, and any wee bits in the newspapers. A memorise a' that.'

'What on earth for?'

'It's quite inter*est*in'.'

'But you said you weren't interested.'

He gave me a worried glance, as though resentful that I wouldn't allow him to mix truth and lies on the same subject. He opted for the truth. 'That's right. Well, the thing is, if A know a' that stuff, it keeps his mind aff the fact that A cannae run, or jump, or be an athlete like him.'

'Have you tried?'

'A've tried. A wis hardly able tae *walk* when he had me

26

tryin'.' He scuffed one foot through the gravel inside the hut. 'It wis nae use. A'm jist no' made for it. Even he had tae admit that A'd never make a success o' it.'

'But you can succeed in other things.'

'Oh, aye! Wance A'm qualified as an accountant he'll be happy.'

'You *do* want to be an accountant?'

'Dae you want tae be an engineer? A mean, really? Is that whit you've always wantit tae be? Or is that whit's wantit fur ye?'

'I didn't think about it much. It's my father's occupation and I expect I'll go into my father's business.'

'Sure.'

'But your father isn't an accountant.'

'Naw. My father's an athlete. No' jist that – he's a good athlete. He wins prizes at it. That's whit makes him so sure o' himsel'. That's whit he was gonnae pass on tae me.'

For several minutes there was only the sound of the rain drumming on the tarred roof as we considered the obligations of only sons to the hopes of their fathers. More pertinently I tried to imagine how irascible my father might have become if I'd turned out to be dull and stupid with no aptitude for engineering when he'd devoted his life to it, largely on my behalf. I began to appreciate Mr Mulvenny's fortitude and spirit when the only possible success in the future depended upon Andy. It was not, after all, that he had unfounded faith in his son. It was more fragile and more tenacious than that. He had unfounded hope. I asked Andy, 'Couldn't your father go in for promotion in the shipyard?'

'Instead, you mean?'

That was what I meant, but said, 'No. As well.'

'That wid be like admittin' that his job wis more important than his runnin'.'

'And isn't it?'

Andy shook his head. 'He knows the job's nothin' special.'

And that, of course, was the motive force of everything in Mr Mulvenny's life. He *was* someone special. There were many charge-hands and foremen and managers in the shipyard. There was only one champion runner. He could do with ease what few men could do at all; and out there, through the downpour, defying the weight of the sodden turf and the hazards of treacherous mud, he was proving it, again. To me, in the snug dry hut, it now seemed less objectionable that at home he was a haughty and irritating despot. His home was just where he kept the emblems of his real identity; and his family.

At the shipyard I very rarely saw him at all, since the engine side was quite a distance from the shipbuilding side. And it was there, in the department which stored and worked all the plating, that Mr Mulvenny was a charge-hand. On one occasion, though, I was sent across there by my foreman with the secret plans of a kitchen wall-cabinet he wanted to have constructed.

'Ask for Andrew Mulvenny,' my foreman said. 'Anybody there will point him out tae ye.'

'I know him.'

'Oh? Well, jist hand him this sketch and tell him it's fae me. He'll know what it is.'

This seemed superfluous since, even at a glance, a child would know what it was. It was a small kitchen cabinet made of aluminium planishing sheets. But what my fore-man meant was that he had a confidential arrangement with Andrew to have the 'home-job' done, and have the time and materials costed to a legitimate customer – probably the Admiralty, which bore the cost of most unexplained expenditure in that and every yard where they were philan-thropic enough to place a contract.

The plate shop was vast and very noisy. Sprawled all over the sanded floor were gargantuan machines which rolled thick cold steel as though it were papier-mâché. There were huge presses, bending machines, and punches which could bite gaping holes in anything that was fed to them. Over-head, hanging from slings or magnets, the cranes bore plates as slender-looking as guillotine blades or as unwieldy as the whole bow section of a ship. Through this giant's playground-in-pandemonium the small figure of Mr Mul-venny strode with purposeful calm and authority. He wore a brown 'smeeky', or dust-coat, which looked as though it was tailor-made. As he approached me I started shouting the message I'd been given. Without pausing he shook his head at me and walked past. Without looking back he beckoned, indicating that I should follow him to a little office which had been sound-proofed by the simple means of covering it with sandbags. There were no windows. It looked exactly like a wartime command-post. Andrew sat at his desk and extended his hand for the sketch.

After a moment he said, 'That seems clear enough. When does he want it?'

'He didn't say.'

'You can tell him it'll be after the week-end.'

'I don't think he wants me to know.'

Andrew leaned back and raised his eyebrows. 'Why's that?'

'Well, I got the impression it was a . . . private arrangement.'

'I don't think he'll care what impression you got, Billy. And I think he'll want to know it'll be ready by Tuesday. So, tell him that. Okay?'

I nodded, then suddenly he sprang up at me; or so I thought as I stumbled back. He lunged out of the door, allowing me to hear what he had already identified. The clamour had increased to include a violent screeching sound. Mr Mulvenny was running towards a group of shouting men gathered at one of the massive rolling mills. A long sheet of thick steel plate which was being drawn into the machine had slipped out of the guides which fed it squarely into the rollers. It was buckling and grinding. The machine operator had jumped clear of his perch as the free edge of the plate reared up at him, blocking the machine controls. There was no way of stopping the machine and the great jaws went on pulling and folding and tearing the plate. The noise was incredible and the mindless violence of it was frightening.

Andrew, alert and on his toes like a boxer squaring up to the inhuman giant opponent, circled round assessing the dangers and the damage. The free edge of the plate was scraping over the control position and crumpling the little handrail which surrounded it. The access ladder had already been chewed into the machine. Andrew took off his dust-coat and lay down on the sand. He wriggled carefully under the plate as it continued to move slowly forward. All we could see was his forearm and his hand gripping the edge of the plate as it started to drag him as well. Only then, when it was too late to stop him, did we realise his intention. Clinging to the back of the plate, he hoped it would pull him near enough to reach the Stop button. If the plate folded inward he would be crushed. If the Stop button was damaged or its effect delayed, he would be too near to avoid falling under the roller. His men watched his progress open mouthed and one was weeping at the sheer bravery of it.

As he edged nearer to the control-box which we could not see, we *could* see blood running down his exposed forearm. He was supporting practically all of his weight with one hand and the edge of the plate was cutting into his palm. Meanwhile, electricians were in a frenzy of activity trying to find the main power point which fed that particular machine. One after another the wrong machines fell silent while the one we were all watching screeched and thundered. Andrew held on and inch by inch the plate continued to buckle outward. Then the roaring stopped. He'd reached the button and it worked. Suddenly deprived of power, the rollers violently regurgitated several feet of twisted plate. It loosened Andrew's grip and threw him clear. Whether he was unconscious or just exhausted I didn't know but he was carried into the little sandbagged office. His trousers were wet and soiled but the men who lifted him cared nothing for that.

I waited around until he recovered. They told me he wanted to see me and when I went into the box he was dressed in dungarees and his hand was bandaged. He beckoned me close so that the others wouldn't hear. 'Billy, ye'll say nothing aboot this at home.'

'But your . . .'

His voice was soft but peremptory. 'Nothing! Okay?'

I nodded and went back to the machine-shop, marvelling that anyone could take such a risk to save a machine. Admittedly, it was a machine worth tens of thousands of pounds but I think Andrew had taken that risk because it was his responsibility; and because he was sure he could do anything he set his mind to. Nor did he ever mention the incident. Though willing to boast about his prowess as a runner, he said not a word about his astonishing courage. But it was saving the machine which got him promotion, whether he wanted it or not. The firm jumped him over the position of foreman to make him a manager.

As soon as he got the much higher wages in his first *monthly* pay cheque he wanted to throw me out. In his view it was bad enough that a charge-hand should take in a lodger. The thought that a *manager* should have one was insufferable. By then I was settled and unwilling to leave. Also, Mrs Mulvenny had got used to me and with Andy only home at week-ends she liked having my company. It was she who suggested a quite subtle formula. 'Tell him you'll move as soon as ye find another place jist as good.' That's what I told Andrew. And occasionally I reported hearing of a vacancy but it did not surprise either of us that such finds never came up to the standard of *his* accommodation.

Young Andy was more fortunate. He'd found lodgings with a saintly old couple in a lane off the Broomielaw. As he told it on his week-end visits, they had to be forced to take the rent and were obsessive about privacy. Not only did they give him a key to *his* room, but securely locked themselves away in their own. Everything was done for him, though he never saw them do it. He was less happy about his studies, however. The Glasgow School of Accountancy was a grimly efficient task-master with a reputation for producing winners. They did this partly by excellence of training but more by their ability to spot losers at a very early stage – and get rid of them. Their students faced a half-term test and a full-term exam in each of the three years of the course. Andy lasted a year.

I knew what news he had brought as soon as he came into the kitchen that Saturday afternoon at lunchtime. His parents, not knowing that such news was possible, were deluded until we had eaten the meal which had been kept waiting for him. I think that was the only time I felt sorry for

Andy. As we ate he replied in the usual way to the usual questions about what was happening in Glasgow and if there had been any sightings of the saintly hermits. Mrs Mulvenny had detailed questions on the serviceability of his socks and underwear. Also, the state of his health. Constant study had made him pale and Mr Mulvenny always wanted a report on the quantity of fresh air taken during the previous week. All these questions were answered and Mr Mulvenny seemed well pleased. 'I think ye've got a bit more colour in ye're face,' he said.

'Well . . . I've had a few days away from the College,' Andy began – trying to get to the point as gently as possible.

'Oh, aye? That's the end of term break, I suppose.'

'In a way, yes.' Andy followed his father in rising from the table.

Mrs Mulvenny was about to eat her meal and I remained seated, sipping my tea very slowly so that she wouldn't be eating alone; though she did not notice that I did so.

'If you had a few days off ye should have come home,' said Andrew.

Andy let that pass and I vividly saw how he had spent those days, walking along the river bank, wandering through the impervious Victorian city, wondering how he was going to tell his father the truth. He caught my eye and his expression was utterly wretched.

'I used to hate end of term,' I said, uselessly.

'So, you'll have had your Exam, then?'

'Yes. We had the Exam last week.'

'*Last* week?'

Andy nodded. 'This week we got the results.'

'I see.' And Mr Mulvenny was just beginning to see.

'They hiv an awful lot o' exams in that place,' Isa observed, her mouth full and her knife busily scraping the plate. She enjoyed her own cooking.

'Well?' asked Mr Mulvenny, ignoring the interruption.

'I didnae . . . pass . . . the Exam.'

'Oh! I'm sorry tae hear that. So, this'll mean another extra year, eh?'

'No.'

'I mean, like ye did your last year at school again. Ye got through fine the second time.'

'No, Da, it's not like that.' His voice had taken on that soft, ingratiating tone I'd so often heard him use to his father – as though he was holding up a cushion to muffle the force of expected anger. 'On Thursday, there, they gave me a letter.' He drew it quickly from the inside pocket of his jacket and gave it to Andrew. But while it was being read he reported on the contents, trying to make the blunt rejection more acceptable. 'They have an awful lot of people wanting tae get intae the College, so they cannae really keep other people on if they don't pass the Exams. It's jist that they don't have the space, y'know, or the staff tae cope wi' . . .'

' "Quite unsuitable",' quoted Mr Mulvenny. 'Did it take them a year tae find out ye were quite unsuitable?'

'Whit's that?' asked Isa, now tuning in to the conversation. And to my astonishment, they did not tell her. They just ignored her question and she did not find that surprising. There was a silence while Mr Mulvenny folded the letter and put it in *his* pocket. 'Whit dae they say?' Isa persisted.

Andrew brushed the question aside. 'It's jist a . . . it's an end of term report. A statement on the curriculum for next term.' He knew his wife would not pursue a word as difficult as 'curriculum'. And he was right. She gave a little grunt of impatience and set about clearing up the table. Andrew then looked directly at his son and promised, 'You're goin' tae be busy next term. And in Glasgow.'

At the time I assumed he meant another accountancy college. Certainly Isa would have no preference between one such establishment or another, and if that could be managed there was no point in alarming her.

'Thanks, Da,' said Andy, clearly amazed at the resilience of his father and no doubt ashamed that he'd been so fearful of breaking the news. What he, and I, had not realised was that the College had slighted not Andy but Andrew by the rejection he now carried. The son was now wholly an extension of his father, and his father – no matter what

33

evidence might be presented – could never be a loser. It was too late for that.

' "Unsuitable"!' Mr Mulvenny repeated the word that rankled. 'How can ye be unsuitable when ye were good enough tae get in tae their College?' None of us could answer that and he went on. 'They found the fees suitable all right.'

'It's jist a matter o' the space. That's how they cannae let students do a year a second time,' Andy repeated to make it more true.

Mr Mulvenny puffed disdainfully. 'For all they've done ye'd have been as well at night-school like Billy, there.'

'How often dae ye go?' Andy asked me, as one unfamiliar with a plebeian ritual.

'Tuesdays and Thursdays here and Fridays at the Tech. in Glasgow.'

He was amazed. 'Ye go up tae Glasgow and back every Friday!'

'Yes.'

Mr Mulvenny shook his head dolefully. 'He's up tae his elbows in grease all day then back and forward on trains all night.'

'That's one reason why I'm going to buy a car,' I told them.

'A *car*!' They exclaimed the words in disbelieving unison. There was no one on that street, or for several streets around, who had a car of their own. There were one or two vans with holes cut in the sides for windows but no real cars. The idea that an apprentice should own a car was indecent.

'I'll be getting it in the spring.'

'What de you want a car for?' asked Mr Mulvenny. 'Ye go nowhere.'

'I will when I have it.'

'Maybe we could go over tae Largs in the summer,' Isa suggested.

'Of course! I'll be able to take you out wherever you want to go.'

'Wherever *we* want to go,' her husband decided, 'we can manage perfectly well on our own.'

'He could take us out to the field events,' Andy offered

and I could see his father had difficulty rejecting that out of hand. But really I didn't care whether or not they found a suitable use for my car. What was important was that, at last, I would be able to insulate myself from strangers.

In the train, I stare up at the blue ceiling-light. It seems to gyrate and recede from me. It brings to mind the blue, flashing light on the roof of the police car.

That came on a stickily warm sunny morning. I was off work because a deep cut in my hand had become infected with lubricating oil. This did not prevent my habitual spare-time activity of repainting the coal box in the lobby. Shortly before lunch-time Mrs Harper called in on Isa before she went on to do some shopping. They were talking in the kitchen about Andy.

Isa told her, 'He comes home at week-ends, of course, but it's no' worth his while travellin' up and down tae Glasgow during the week.'

'How long will he be at this er . . .'

'Secretarial College.'

'Aye.'

'Another two years, if he passes the exams, that is.' She felt it wise to add this rider because young Andy had been 'unlucky' a few times by now.

'I expect he will,' said Ella. 'They're sure tae be easier than them he had for the accountants.' She eased the straps of her brassiere off the red patches of her shoulders. 'How can ye stick the heat in here, Isa. And the smell o' that paint! Will ye no' open the winda?'

'Oh, certainly.' She leaned over the cluttered sink and hefted the frame up as far as it would go. 'But I think the air's warmer outside than it is in.'

'Ooooph! That's better. Just as long as there's some movement.' Ella unbuttoned her blouse and flapped it a few times. 'Still, it must be funny, not havin' Andy in the house, I mean.'

'Aye. And even though it's best for him, still, it's a worry.'

'A'm sure. Knowin' what Glasgow's like.'

'It's no' that so much. It's just . . . I'm that used tae doin' for them, y'know? Sometimes I just forget, like . . . he'll no' be in for his tea – and I make it. Then Andrew thinks I'm complainin'.'

Ella had her own views on how Isa should deal with Andrew's complaining but from years of fruitless advice and example knew there was no use in mentioning them. She changed the subject and lowered her voice – though not enough. 'Ye've still got yer ludger, though?'

'Oh, aye!' Isa stage-whispered. 'An' he's awful considerate. That's a change, tae. Aye, Billy's a big help tae me wi' Andrew out so much.'

The sound of the ambulance passing at speed, bell jangling, cut through the other traffic sounds which rose from the street through the open window.

'I thought he'd stopped the runnin',' said Ella.

'That's right. For over a year now. But he's out practically every night coachin' – trainin' the younger ones, y'know.'

'He's a right go-ahead man, your Andrew,' Ella had to concede.

'He is that!'

'I could have done wi' somebody like him instead-a Joe.'

Isa shook a spoon at her in friendly reproval. 'Now, Ella, that's not right. Joe's very . . . cheery.'

'Aye, wi' a bucket in 'im.'

'He's a good turn.'

'On the piana – that's aboot a'.' She wriggled uncomfortably. 'And we havenae even got a piana.'

They lapsed into silence for several long moments, considering the merits of their respective husbands and gradually it occurred to Isa that in all the time she'd known the Harpers, one obvious question had never been answered.

'Ella? What does Joe *do*, exactly?'

'Do? How d'ye mean, "do"?' Any irritation in her voice was more due to the heat than the question.

'What does he do for work, I mean.'

'He does withoot, maist o' the time,' said Ella. 'When we got married, he was a welder – or, so he claimed. Since then I have no idea, but whatever it is, he gets

36

money for it. I believe he helps bookies a lot.'

'Andrew doesnae approve o' gamblin',' Isa reported.

'Naw. There's a helluva lot Andrew doesnae approve o',' her friend observed, unabashed. She writhed in a struggle with her underclothes. 'Holy God! These things are stickin' tae me. I'd better go the messages before A melt. An' it'll be worse goin' oot in the efternoon.'

'I don't think I'll bother today wi' messages.'

'Well,' said Ella, sensing evasion, 'if you're no' goin' oot, is there anything I can get ye?'

'I don't think so, Ella. I think I'll just . . . er . . .'

'Make do?'

Isa laughed at being so easily caught out. 'That's it! Must do's a good master, and make do's his wife.'

'Aye, but first ye should make sure – what there is,' retorted Ella. 'You're a soft-mark, Isa. I've told ye that before. It's wan thing I'll say for Joe – when he's got it I always get the most of it.'

'I'm sure ye do.'

'Damn right!'

'It's no' that I don't get enough money,' Isa said, and believed it. 'The thing is A'm no' a very good manager. Time and again Andrew's showed me how A could've managed better.'

'Oh, aye?'

'He's awful good at figures, Andrew.'

'Figures, tae!' said Ella, but tempered the sarcasm in her voice just enough to avoid bringing it to Isa's attention.

'A think that's how young Andy got interested in accountancy – hearin' us talkin' aboot money.'

'He'd be able tae hear that well enough in his room, I expect.'

I went out carrying the can of waste turpentine to empty it in the wash-house drain. At the bottom of the stair I almost ran into a policeman and beyond him, framed in the close-mouth, I saw the police car with its flashing blue light. The policeman asked me which landing the Mulvennys lived on, then told me why he wanted to know. He was a young constable and obviously glad to find somebody else who could break the news.

37

The women turned at the sound of the front door slamming and were startled to see me burst into the kitchen. Several details imprinted themselves on my mind. Mrs Mulvenny standing in front of the sink at the window, looking over her shoulder at me; like a tall, ungainly bird alarmed by a predator. And Mrs Harper, half sprawled on a chair, her legs stretched out and her blouse unbuttoned all down the front. I was glad she was there. Unskilled in the niceties of social occasions, she was a woman of resilience in a crisis.

Having caught my breath, I began, 'Mrs Mulvenny . . .'

'Billy! What is it?' Her voice was maddeningly far from suiting what I knew to be the occasion.

Ella focused much more accurately. 'What's up, son? Ye're as white as a sheet.'

'There's a police car . . .'

'Police!' Isa turned right round, but slowly, and took a step towards me.

Ella scrambled to her feet. 'Whit dae they want ye fur?' Then, coming immediately to my defence, 'I'll talk tae them.'

'No. Not me. They've come to take Mrs Mulvenny to the hospital.'

Ella knew at once why. 'Aw, Isa! It's Andrew.'

'My Andrew? Oh.'

I forced myself to go on. 'An accident in the plate-shop. They asked me to tell you and they . . . the police are waiting to take you to the hospital.'

'Oh, God! Is he bad?'

'They said he . . . I don't know. Car's waiting . . . now! They'll take you.'

'No.'

Ella, for whom time had not come to a halt, tried to reason with her. 'They've got Andrew in the hospital, Isa. You'll have to go. He'll want to see you.'

'Go? Like this?' With an attitude of wonder she gazed down at the floral, and stained, wrap-around pinafore she was wearing.

'Please, Mrs Mulvenny!'

She tried, yet again, to assimilate the separate factors

which should not be any of her business. 'The police. Andrew in hospital. Car waitin'.' Then she came to me and stared close into my face – as though, after all, she would see I was lying. She saw I was not lying and said, 'Will you come?'

'Do you want me wi' ye, Isa?' asked Ella.

Mrs Mulvenny shook her head, still staring at me. 'Billy, will you come? I cannae go ma'sel. You come wi' me.' Then she picked her way out of the room and down the stairs, exactly as she was, and without looking back.

I didn't know what to do. And, at eighteen, that incompetence bothered me a lot. Later, I realised the main thing I had to do was – be there.

Andrew had been crushed under a steel plate when a crane-sling broke. It was several days before we knew whether or not he would live. Isa spent those days waiting in hospital corridors. She refused to eat. It was when they told her Andrew had started to recover that she collapsed – a result of delayed shock, relief and fatigue. What they did not tell her was that Andrew's legs would remain paralysed. He had been told but, with that maddening composure which was close to arrogance, this was something else he kept from his wife when we were able to visit him for the first time. The healthy colour and shine on his skin were gone from his face but his eyes were as sharp and bright as ever.

'Hello, Isa! Billy!'

Mrs Mulvenny bumped heavily against the corner of the foot of the bed in her eagerness to reach him. 'Andrew!' She was smiling and weeping at once. 'A've been here all the time but they wouldnae let me in till now.'

'Aye. They told me.' His voice was very weak. 'What have ye brought me?'

'Oh, not much. Billy's got it in the bag there.'

I laid out the usual array of fruit juice, fruit and magazines, then retired to a position notionally out of range of whatever private conversation they might wish to have.

'That's very nice,' said Andrew. 'Next time ye come ye could bring the local paper. I want tae keep up tae date wi' what the club's doin'.'

'When'll they let ye oot?'

'That'll no' be for a while yet.'

'A'll come an' visit ye whenever they'll let me,' Isa promised.

'No, no. Once a week will be fine,' Andrew decided firmly. 'One o' the firm's directors is comin' tae see me the morra. His secretary phoned them.'

'Fancy that! Still, it wis a terrible thing tae happen and A suppose they feel a wee bit responsible.' She was uncertain of that, but repeated, 'A terrible business altogether.'

Andrew shook his head impatiently and smiled. 'Not so terrible. One thing's sure, Andy's goin' tae be all right now.'

Mrs Mulvenny could see no connection in these remarks but I saw the clear line to financial compensation. When he said that, his voice had something of its old assurance. He knew that, even if he was going to be a cripple for the rest of his life, he would win.

It was the ward sister who told Isa about the paralysis; in a whispered conversation as we were leaving after a visit. On the bus going home she was very quiet and, suspecting why, I did not prompt her. As we were nearing the playing-fields she voiced the end of what must have been a commentary she'd been running in her mind.

'We'll have more time th'gither, that's wan thing,' she said.

'What?'

'Wi' him no' able tae get out at all, we'll have more time th'gither than we've ever had before. I'll be glad o' *that*, at least.' She turned to me. 'And if we have that, nothin' else can go wrong, can it?'

'No. I'm sure everything will be all right.'

Finding herself without the strict day-to-day guidance of her husband, Mrs Mulvenny cautiously, then whole-heartedly, expanded her interests. She took a job. Working with other people gave her a jaunty assurance she'd never had before. Now she and I sat down to the table at the same time and she'd tell me about her day.

'They lassies at the shop have me in stitches! And the things they don't know wid fill a book.'

40

'What sort of things?'

'Never mind. Things you've nae right to know.' She laughed. 'But I keep them right – or thin, at least!'

'Oh!' I was embarrassed. How was it, I wondered, that whenever one joked with women they always seemed to think it was a joke about sex.

'They're awful nice lassies, though,' Isa went on. 'Y'know, it's the first time I've thought it would have been fine tae have a daughter instead o' a son. Of course, Mr Mulvenny was quite set on havin' a son – tae be good at the sort o' thing he likes.'

'Yes.'

She at once purged this faintly disloyal thought, 'I'm just mentionin' that the lassies make me think o' that. Everybody really wants a son and Andy's a fine boy. He'll make a good husband for some lucky lassie.'

'Yes.'

'So wid you! You're such a great help in the hoose. When are you gonnae start coortin'?'

She smiled across the table at me. This was a theme to which she'd returned time and again during the winter that Andrew was in hospital. It seemed to worry her that I didn't have any 'dates' and occasionally, when I took *her* to the pictures, she behaved with uncharacteristic and wholly misplaced tact, thinking that I'd been stood up by some girl and that she was filling a painful breach. I made it as plain as I could that she wasn't standing in for anybody but she interpreted my insistence as evidence of hurt and tried harder than ever to make me enjoy myself. In April, though, I did have something encouraging to report to her.

'I shall be having my tea early on Thursday, Mrs Mulvenny.'

'Oh, yes?'

'I'm going to see "The Inn of the Sixth Happiness".'

'Is that a picture?'

'Yes. It's based on a book called "The Small Woman" but they got a very tall woman to play it.'

She sensed some disapproval in this and rather sharply observed, 'Well, we cannae all be small and neat.'

'Or Ingrid Bergman, for that matter.'

Isa let that pass and fastened on the more important aspect. 'Ye're no' goin' by yersel again, are ye?'

'No. I'm taking a girl called Elsie.'

'Oh, ho!'

'Yes. And we have some things to discuss first, so I'd like to have my tea early.'

'Things tae discuss?' To her that meant one of two things; an unwanted pregnancy or an imminent engagement. She had to tread warily. 'Ye never let on there was somethin' serious in the wind.'

'I only met her a couple of weeks ago.'

That was disappointing. Nothing serious could be obvious or arrived at in a couple of weeks, so she went on to relate the latest hilarious happenings at the wool shop.

The money she made at the shop was needed. For though the shipyard eventually paid Andrew a lump sum in compensation, it all went to Andy. He was to be set up in business. That meant he didn't really have to continue slogging at the secretarial college. There was no need. He became a sort of Insurance Broker. He'd opened an office by the time Andrew was ready to leave hospital and drew himself away from the City long enough to accompany his father home in the ambulance.

In the sleeping compartment, once more in motion, I switch on the bunk-light and open the new pack of cigarettes provided by the attendant. I know I'll need them. The lighter flame is startlingly yellow against the neon glow. And I leave the light on. If I'm going to face that homecoming again, I can't do it in the dark.

I waited with Isa in a sparkling, spring-clean atmosphere that Saturday morning. In the lobby, the brand new wheel-chair, glinting with chrome, reflected the gleam of silver trophies on the sideboard. Even the coal-box, covered with a length of bright curtain material, was passing disguised as a hall-table. And, of course, Isa herself was wearing a new frock. It was deep cream-coloured in jersey material with long puffed sleeves gathered tightly at the wrist. Yes, everything was ready; over ready. It had been for days, during which her excitement and gauche high spirits had grown to a hectic pitch of expectation.

Then, about half an hour before Andrew was due, she decided to cut her hair.

'Why?' I asked her, more than a little irritated because I, as chief helper in all the preparations, had decided that positively nothing else could be done. She was in my room bending down to look in the triple mirrors of the dressing-table.

She sighed, 'Well, I've had it this way for ages. And ma face's got thinner. You don't mind if I cut it in here? You've got the mirrors where I can see the back.'

'I like it the way it is.'

'Aye, but you don't hiv tae sort it up every mornin'. Look! See the length of it! He must be sick of the sight o' me like this. I've had my hair the same way since we got married. Of course, it was all the "go" then – plaited and coiled, y'know. Like Mrs Simpson.'

'Who?'

'Mrs Simpson.'

'I don't know a Mrs Simpson.'

'Aye, ye *dae*. Her that married the King.' Isa began shearing off long strands of glossy auburn hair. 'Of course, she changed it after a while. But I kept it the same. Made me look no' sa tall, ye know, drawn down on my ears.' She chuckled as she peered into the mirrors to see what havoc she was causing at the back. 'Andrew made me wear flat shoes for the weddin' photographs. Quite right. It's that silly lookin' if the woman's bigger than the man – in a photograph, anyway. That ye're gonnae keep!' The strict logic of this line of thought defies explanation, but it made sense to me then, the way Isa said it. And she went on, 'I must say I always liked him – the Prince a' Wales. And they had a very happy marriage. Like us, in a way.' She surveyed the effect, so far, and sighed with satisfaction – whether at her skill as a hairdresser or at the continuing success of the Windsors, I didn't know.

Having rid herself of the sheer length of hair she now set about the idea of styling and vigorously wielded a comb. 'That's a chuggy bit,' she said, wrenching the comb free, then returned to Edward VIII and his lady. 'Pity they never had any weans, though. I'd have liked tae have more, but after the bother I had wi' Andy they gave me a big operation. If we'd had a few more sons, wan o' them might have went in for sports. Andrew would have liked that.' She ducked forward to catch my eye in the mirror. 'Have I got that straight? These scissors are no' much use. It wastes them, cuttin' up the cardboard tae light the fire. Still, bein' an only son means he has a' the better chance. He'll do well, the same boy. Just you wait!'

This meant that whereas she and Mr Mulvenny never had any doubts about Andy's prospects she was acknowledging that I may have been puzzled by his several choices of career when, for some reason, he didn't pass particular exams. That was all changed by the compensation money and now everything was clear ahead.

'Gi'es ye somethin' tae look forward tae in yer old age,' she said. 'Nothing should be spared for yer own.' There was a pause filled by the sound of random snipping, then she concluded, 'You know, I think she was bigger than him, tae – that Mrs Simpson.'

We were interrupted by the slamming of car doors in the street and I ran to the open kitchen window. Having caught the Mulvenny habit I turned back into the room and shouted, 'That's the ambulance now!'

Isa's excited voice called, 'Well, shut the winda in case he looks up!'

When I rejoined her in my room she had bundled all the shorn hair into a newspaper and was heading for the kitchen fire to burn it. 'Shall I go down?'

'Naw, you wait here. The ambulance men'll carry him up and there's no' much room on the stair. Oh, I'd better move these rugs so he can wheel the chair in. Is that everything, noo?'

'Everything's fine.'

'Are ye sure the chair's handy in the lobby, there?'

'Yes, I've . . .'

Suddenly, consternation smote her. 'Whit's that smell? Oh, my God – the stew.' She ran into the kitchen wailing, 'I knew there was something. Did ye no' see that smoke?'

'Maybe it's your hair,' I shouted.

'Is it Hell! It's the stew.'

I waited for her to return from the kitchen but before she could complete her salvage operation we heard the front door open and the ambulance party bumping against things in the lobby. Andy's voice asked, 'Is that all right, Dad?' I went to help them.

Andy looked beyond me. 'Is the place on fire?'

'No,' his father grunted. 'It's the dinner burned, I expect.'

'Can you manage through to the front room?' asked Andy. He meant my room. And he totally ignored the two ambulance men who'd carried his father up six flights of stairs. They turned and left without a word.

'I can manage fine,' said Mr Mulvenny. 'Fine. Don't shove me. Where's your mother?'

'She's in the kitchen,' I told them.

Isa!' he shouted, and wheeled himself unerringly into my room. Obviously he'd done a lot of practice in chair-manoeuvring at the hospital.

Mrs Mulvenny called back, gurgling slightly with pleasure. 'Here, Andrew. I'm just putting the water in the pot.' Then she appeared, flushed and happy, in the doorway. Mr Mulvenny wheeled the chair in a neat arc to face her. 'Andrew! It's great tae have ye back,' she said.

'What have you done with your hair?' he asked in a voice that was contracted like a tight fist.

'Do you like it? I thought I needed a change.'

Andrew gathered himself and spat venomously, 'You look like a bloody clown!'

In the train, at a heart-mended distance of time and miles from that scene, I still find it necessary to reach for my handkerchief and mop up. An express rushing in the opposite direction seems to rake our train with heavy machine-gun fire as it passes and I rock on my feet. I slide open the silencing shutter then put out the light so that I can watch the amorphous shapes of the scenery whip past under a cloudy sky. There is something ridiculous about sleeping coaches, as Norman MacCaig said; about stretching yourself on a shelf to be carried sideways through the night. Increasingly, my shelf this night is becoming something of a rack. I try to recall the really happy times, for me at the Mulvennys', and realise – with dismay – that they'd all been when Andrew was in hospital and Andy was living in Glasgow. They were when Isa was working in the wool shop. She was such a cheerful woman and had an intricate way of thinking which I found fascinating. Other people, too, found her cheerful, but also muddled and vague. They did not take the trouble to follow her line of thought or, perhaps, were certain that their own line of thought was the only one to follow. They, of course, were much older than I and had the experience to confirm such a time-saving prejudice. Isa's conversation delighted me.

During that 'free' period she did not feel guilty of thinking primarily of herself, or of enjoying it. Andrew was being cared for in hospital – which was as it should be. Young Andy was full of plans and busy in Glasgow – which was as they'd always hoped. And there she was – gossiping with willing customers at the wool shop, sharing hilarious secrets with the sales-girls and earning 'good money' on her own account. At home her only duty was looking after a young English lodger who enjoyed a strange lapse of pride in thinking it natural that he should do many of the household chores. Isa could hardly wait for Andrew to come home so that he could see how much she had improved herself in assurance and capability.

In the event, he was not impressed. Indeed, he found her remarkable growth in assurance extremely irritating, since it seemed designed to emphasise his sudden lack of use as an athlete and as a worker. If the Harpers had remained in the neighbourhood Ella may have seen to it that Mrs Mulvenny did not give up any of her gains. But Ella and Joe had been among the first to be rehoused, away from the steadily deteriorating area where the Mulvennys lived. And Isa had to give in – without being really aware of what she was losing.

Joe Harper did make very occasional visits to the invalid, if only to keep his hand in at the piano in my room. One day I came back and, before I'd reached the second landing, heard the familiar Charlie Kunz style with the tune 'It Happened In Monterey'. I opened the front door softly and waited in the lobby, feeling that I couldn't very well barge in on my landlord and his guest – even though they were occupying the room I rented.

Andrew was saying, 'I can rely on you for all the old favourites, Joe. And all the old times.'

'The old times were the best times,' replied the pianist, strumming. 'I always mind the parties we used tae have here. For you.'

'For all of us. Those were the days. You and Ella and . . .'

Joe interrupted eagerly. 'And another bit o' champion silver on the sideboard.'

'Aye, aye. Now all I can do is sit here at the window and watch them playin' bloody cricket across in the park, there.'

'Cricket, eh?'

'In the summer, nothing else. In the winter, nothing at all.'

'Heh, heh, heh,' chuckled Joe tactically. His attention remained fixed on the missing silver. I was sitting on the bare top of the sideboard. It had been bare for many months. 'Cricket, eh? Ye'll no' win many trophies for that.'

'Still, this is better than the kitchen window, lookin' onto the street.'

Joe tried again. 'I notice ye've moved the trophies.' There was a pause. He continued, 'I mean, off the lobby sideboard, er . . .'

'What?'

'Your cups and shields and that. Have ye got them stored away somewhere?'

'I got rid of them. Oh, aye. Too many memories.'

'Of course. I can understand that.'

'Got rid of the lot.'

'Uh huh.' Joe tried another ploy. 'Young Andy wid take them, I expect. Eh? Now that he's got a house of his own. He was always very proud of his old man.'

'It's very nice, I believe,' said Andrew, modestly re-

47

strained. 'We havenae seen it yet, but his wife and him seem to be pleased wi' it.'

'Oh, it's a nice area, that. Ella was sayin', they'll be expectin' us for a visit. Now they've settled.'

'I'm sure they'd like to see you.'

'We'll hiv tae get the address . . .' He paused. His friend did not respond. 'The exact address . . . ye know.'

'Aye.'

But Mr Mulvenny had no intention of giving him any address, exact or fanciful, and I decided I'd spent enough time hovering in the lobby. I pushed open the door and marched in. 'Oh, I'm sorry. I didn't know you were here, Mr Harper.'

Joe welcomed me. 'Come in, son. Come in. Nice tae see ye. You been tae the library?'

'No. These are my text books. I'm studying for the H.N.C.'

'We'll no' disturb you,' said Mr Mulvenny without turning his chair which was set at the window. 'We're just havin' a quiet chat. There's plenty of space.'

I moved to a corner of the room, dumped my books noisily on a table and gave the impression of setting immediately to work. Mr Mulvenny was dressed as fully and neatly as he was always dressed. He wore a clean shirt with a suitable tie and a well-pressed suit with a waistcoat. He dressed himself. His shoes were polished and his chair was polished. He did those himself, too. Every morning he emerged like that from what had been Andy's room and wheeled himself around all day, like a coiled spring. The change in sleeping arrangements was made as soon as he came back from hospital. Mrs Mulvenny now had the 'set-in' kitchen bed to herself, Mr Mulvenny had Andy's room as impregnable home-base and I, it seemed, shared the front room with anyone who was passing.

'What was I sayin'?' asked Mr Mulvenny, when the sounds of my intrusion had subsided.

Joe still had Andy's address in mind. 'You were sayin' about the boy's . . .'

'That's right. The boys' club I used to train. Folded up. Another season finished wi' no coachin' whatsoever . . .

and they came nowhere. So – they've had tae pack it in. Saw that in the paper.'

Joe saw that the conversation needed extra lubrication. He stated boldly, 'Andrew, I'm not surprised. Ever since you had tae stop they've been headin' nowhere. They've got nobody wi' your experience – that's the point.' That, indeed, was Andrew's point and his old crony came to it more readily than most. 'Nobody near as good.'

'Maybe so.'

'No "maybe" about it! That club depended on you.'

'There might be something in that. I mean, there's got to be somebody the young lads can trust . . .'

'. . . look up to . . .'

'Somebody who's proved he knows what it takes.'

Scribbling in my corner I, reluctantly, had to concede the truth of that situation, however artfully presented. Mr Mulvenny had been an excellent coach, as he'd been an excellent athlete. Also, to most strangers outside his home, he was firm, equable and trustworthy. Yes, yes, I thought impatiently, 'outside'. But for a long time now he had not been outside; and I knew the inside target on which he let loose the strain that imposed. Lying in bed at nights I heard his shouting and her sobbing. I heard the doors bang and worse, the silences followed by what had become a dreadful sound – the sucking of the rubber wheels on the polished floor of the lobby before the foot-rest of his chair bumped against my door. Then he would wheel himself in and start on his addictive recall of past triumphs. Many, many, many evenings I had to sit there trying feverishly to study while he repeated long, rambling stories; many passages of which I knew by heart. Like the one he was telling Joe:

'I mind the time . . . now . . . when was it? The second season, I think. Aye. The second season I ran for them . . . and this is a very good example of the experience ye come tae rely on. Of course, I'd been runnin' for a top outfit on the other side o' the City for years before that . . . and they werenae very pleased when I left them . . . but just the second season after I came here . . .'

'They were very lucky tae get you,' said Joe in an alert, but I knew futile, effort to stem the tide.

'Well – it was handy, y'know. And this race that second season . . .'

'What time is that?' asked Joe, looking sharply at the clock on the mantlepiece.

'Aw, ye've plenty of time, Joe. They don't open for another half-hour. I'd offer ye somethin' tae eat, but I don't know what she's doin'.'

Joe was genuinely surprised. 'Isa! Is she no' at work?'

'Certainly not!' Andrew coiled even tighter. 'I soon put a stop tae that caper. No wife o' mine is gonnae be servin' in a shop.'

'Oh! Well, then, if she's in I must have a word wi' Isa.'

From my corner, I spoke up to forestall this. 'I think she's busy at the moment. Would you like me to make you some tea?'

'Busy?' hissed Andrew. 'What d'ye mean, "busy"? What the hell is there for her tae be "busy" at? Sit where ye are!'

'It's no trouble, I'll just . . .'

His voice was suddenly throaty with anger. 'Sit on yer arse! This is still my house, remember. And we don't want tae interfere wi' your studies.' He shouted, 'Isa!' And I could picture her in the kitchen, jerking sharply with fear.

'Mrs Mulvenny isn't very well,' I said.

Andrew's lips apparently smiled as he stared at me, 'Oh, that's news. She can still walk, I suppose?'

Joe tried to mediate. 'Now, Andrew, if she's no' feelin' well I don't want to . . .'

'Isa! Come here!' shouted Andrew, much louder.

'I'll see if she's any better,' I said, and strode out of the room.

Andrew continued to shout, 'It's none o' your bloody business!' Then he confided loudly to Joe, 'Honest tae God! Sometimes I think I'm the lodger.'

'The lad means well, Andrew.'

'He doesnae mean well by me. It's always her side he takes.'

I urged Isa toward the front room. Her voice was slurred and mumbling. 'I'ss all right, son. I'ss all right, I can manage fine. You put on the kettle.' She went in to face the men. 'Joe! I thought I heard the piana, but it was . . . but then I thought . . . maybe I was just dreamin'. Nice tae see you.'

Joe spread his arms theatrically. 'Hello, Isa!'

'Is, er . . . ' she focused, with effort, to recall the name, 'Ella. Did Ella come wi' ye? Havenae seen Ella for . . . oooh . . . for a long time. Awful kind woman, Ella.'

'Naw, she didnae come. This is her day for the Bingo.'

'Oh, aye. Never tried the Bingo. Crowds frequent them, though.' She sighed. 'Terrible crowded . . . places, I believe.'

'I was just leavin', Isa. Got tae get back, ye know.'

Isa adjusted her stance to take in his standing up. 'Aw, wha' a' shame. Ye could have played us a wee tune . . . '

'I'll see ye again before long, I expect.'

' . . . played us "The Rose a' Tralee", maybe.'

'Sure.' Joe headed for the door. 'Sure. I'll drop in again. See you again, Andrew. Cheerio, for now.'

Isa was having trouble keeping pace with the movement. 'Thought I was dreamin' when I heard the . . . Cheerio! Say to Ella that I was . . . '

The front door slammed.

' . . . askin' for her.'

Andrew, who had contained his fury until Joe was out of range now ran his chair forward as though he might run it into his wife where she stood, swaying slightly. His strong, packed voice lashed at her. 'You're a disgrace! Look at the state you're in. Get out of my sight . . . '

'Andrew! What's wrong?'

' "What's wrong?" ' He aped her soft, slurred speech then went on in his own outraged tones. 'Ye're drunk ya gawky bitch, that's what's wrong. And that shifty wee bastard, Joe Harper, will see that everybody knows it. You don't care about that. Drunk, at this time o' day, and where ye got the money, God only knows! When I've had tae sell all ma silver, and pinch and scrape for no more than decency, you can afford tae buy drink.'

'Naw, Andrew. It was a present. It was money I got as a present.'

He snorted in disbelief. 'Who'd gi'e *you* a present?'

'The boy.'

'Andy?'

'Naw, Billy. He gave me thirty shillin's. That's where I got it. That's true. That's where I got it, Andrew. A wee present.'

'For what?'

'For ma birthday.'

'And you throw it away on drink!'

The enormity of this seemed to affect Isa too. She slumped on a chair and tested the truth to see if it still made a reasonable excuse. 'Well, Andy's away, y'see and I don't . . . I don't get out that much, now. It makes ye feel a bit cheerier, for a wee while.'

'That's enough. We'll have no more o' that. Don't you ever let me see you in that state again.'

'I'm all right.'

'You're a disgrace. Nae wonder yer son cannae stand the sight o' ye.' He'd known from the outset he was going to say that. It was just a matter of choosing the right moment. And he chose well. The woman crumpled completely.

'Naw, Andrew. That's no' true.'

'It is true. Why else d'ye think we've never been asked to their new house? And I don't blame them.'

I pushed open the door and came into the room carrying a tray with the tea things. Andrew turned on me. 'And you're as bad, encouraging her. Well, I hope ye're satisfied wi' the result.' He wheeled the chair smartly about to the open door. 'I'm goin' tae ma bed, and I don't want to hear another word.'

'I'll come an' help ye,' Isa offered, starting to rise.

'You! Help me? When have you ever been a help tae me?'

When he'd gone, I asked her, 'Do you want some tea?'

'What? Oh, tea! That's very nice.'

I poured the tea, put in milk and sugar and stretched to hand her the cup. But she was preoccupied and, raising her hand to her head, knocked the cup on the floor. 'Oooh, sorry. My goodness, look at that! I'm sorry.'

'It's all right. I'll clean it up.'

'Sorry . . . I didnae notice the . . . sorry. But that is not true. No.'

'What?'

'It's not Andy's fault. Not ma Andy. I'm sure he wants tae see me.'

'Oh?' I started mopping up the tea with my handkerchief.

'It's his wife.' But even then, allowances had to be made. 'Of course, she's used tae a better class o' people altogether.'

'Is she?'

'Stands tae reason, that. People want people they're used to. I widnae know whit tae say tae her.'

'I could think of a few things.'

'Ah, but you're different. You're her kind, y'see.' She forgot about the tea and got up to wander back into the kitchen, murmuring, 'Education's the thing.'

As the months went on, things became more and more tense at the Mulvennys'. Finally, I decided I would have to see Andy. I called him at his office and could hardly believe it was him when he came on the line. His voice was much deeper, of course, but his accent had 'improved' quite remarkably. 'Ah, Bill! Yes. You really must come out and see us some afternoon.' He gave me the address which Joe had coveted in vain. This was, indeed, a 'select area' and his modern bungalow was set in a fairly large, well cultivated garden. As it happened, only Andy was there to greet me. He led me out to a table on a small patio so that we could enjoy the sun.

'I hoped I'd have the chance to meet your wife,' I said.

'Yes. She should be back around five. Just having her routine check-up at the clinic.'

'Is she unwell?'

'The natal clinic,' he smiled modestly. 'She does want to meet you.'

'I don't think I can wait until five,' I said.

'That's a pity.'

'Yes. But it'll take me more than an hour to get back to Greenock and I told your mother to expect me at six.'

He shrugged. 'I don't suppose it'll matter much to her when you get back.'

'Yes, it does. And it matters to me, even more.'

'Oh!' He was surprised at my tone. 'I just meant that she was always a bit careless about time.'

'Not about the time to have a meal ready,' I reminded him.

Both of us looked away for a moment over the tidy green suburb and listened to the birds in the trees which lined this 'young executive' avenue. Then I glanced covertly at the expression of relaxed satisfaction on Andy's face. He had turned into a lean, handsome young man and his black hair was trimmed in the most fashionable cut.

'Would you like a drink?' he asked.

'No, thank you.' I was holding myself in decent check, waiting for a chance to pour out my grievances. But what if there was no chance? In this calm, civilised conversation, how could I force the matter on his attention? Again, and for a longer period, we gazed over the gardens.

'You know,' Andy said, 'I've often wondered why you went on living in that house. Especially since she's become so . . . '

'Your mother, you mean?'

He gave me a sharp, puzzled look. 'What's the matter with you? It seems there's nothing I can say but you jump on it.'

'Maybe because you don't say what I expect to hear. It seems to me you don't know what's going on in that house.'

'My father writes to me regularly,' he stated. Then added admiringly, 'Isn't it marvellous the way he's managed to keep his spirit – trapped like that in a wheel-chair?'

'Yes.'

'And on top of that, having to cope with h . . . – my mother. Well . . . you must know that she's started drinking.'

'I know nothing of the kind. She drank too much – once, eight months ago, on her birthday. And he's never let her forget it.'

'She may hide it from you, but it's my father has to put up with her ways.'

'What?' I asked very quietly, and felt like hitting him.

'I mean, she was always very slovenly – but now! If it

54

hadn't been for Dad, God knows where I would have ended up.'

'Listen, Andy, if you don't do something about your – "Dad" – I know where *she'll* end up. In a lunatic asylum. That man is driving your mother to desperation.'

It was impossible for him to believe me. 'My father is an invalid.'

I gathered my breath and stood up; then began pacing round him, and the colourful sunshade, and the white table. 'Sure. Your father is an invalid and I'm sorry for that. But everything he has lost, he's taking out on her. Invalid or not, he has a vicious tongue and he can make her life a misery because . . . she still thinks the world of him. *And* you. She thinks there's nobody like you, either. That's why I came. To ask you . . . Invite your mother here. For a holiday. She needs a break. You owe her that, surely. And I . . . I'm sick to my gut of seeing her hiding behind doors and scared to make a sound, unless he speaks to her first.'

Andy stared up at me, and the light filtering through the sunshade glowed as bars of colour on his crisp white shirt. 'This is none of your business,' he said.

'My business?' I asked incredulously and leaned forward, resting my hands on the table. 'I live there. I've lived there for nearly five years and watched that woman . . . Christ Almighty!' I swung wildly away from him. 'If it's not my business tell me whose business it is; for – somebody – must do something!'

'Well, it's not your place, for a start. And I resent . . .'

I interrupted him, but softly – very softly now, because I dare not alienate him, for Isa's sake. I sat beside him. 'Andy . . . Andy, she is scared to lift a tea-cup with one hand, in case she drops it and the whole day is ruined.'

I close the silencing shutter on the train window again and, for a few moments, it does seem to be effective. And there is nothing to see anyway, or guess at, for we have reached the high hills of Cumbria and the line runs through long sections of deep cuttings which are no more diverting than tunnels. Staring at the strict confines of the sleeping-compartment, I think it must surely have expanded to accommodate the rooms and spaces I knew as an apprentice. Surely my memory has seeped out and filled this impersonal swaying box. Uncharitably, I hope that the next person who occupies it will have as little sleep as I've had; and be haunted by insistent images of perfect strangers. My eyes retain the blur of coloured light on the stark whiteness of Andy's shirt.

Soon afterwards I started my final year by moving into the drawing office. About the only person who was glad of my elevation was Mr Mulvenny. It impressed him that I'd joined the ranks of those who never need to get their hands dirty. And he was glad the neighbours could see his lodger going to work in suit, collar and tie. Mrs Mulvenny worried about the sharp increase in clean shirts to be provided and suggested that maybe if she just washed the collars it would save ironing the entire shirt again. She'd become very nervous of ironing because of the tremor which had developed in her hands; and because of her husband's complaints about *his* shirts. It was an issue that became inflated out of all proportion to its significance and led to a bitter weekly shouting-match. After one such bout I waited until Isa was alone, trying to improve her ironing in the kitchen.

I interrupted her very softly. 'Mrs Mulvenny!'

'What's wrong, son?' Nowadays all her conversations seemed to start with something that was wrong. She hastily placed the iron on its rest.

'Nothing. Nothing's wrong. It's just that I've been thinking it might be more . . . convenient . . . for you if I sent some of my clothes to a laundry.'

'A *laundry*!' She'd never sent anything to a laundry in her life.

'Just to save time, you know.'

'I see.' Her tone indicated that she was not offended or hurt, just resigned to yet another of the large and small changes that kept intruding on her life.

'I'll take a bundle in each week and then collect them.'

'Jist as ye like, Billy.'

'You can make up the bundle for me and maybe you could put in Mr Mulvenny's shirts as well.'

She leaned back, tilted her head to the side and gave me a slow smile. Now she saw what I was doing and why; and was grateful. 'Get the laundry tae dae them as well?'

'I'll pay for the lot,' I assured her.

'Right ye are,' she said, accepting this secret pact. Then, to my surprise, she managed a broad wink. 'Mr Mulvenny will think A've fairly improved.'

I nodded. 'Yes, he will.' But if he did he never mentioned it.

There was no holiday for Isa that summer and in the autumn I left the shipyard to start my time at sea. I gave her the itinerary for the trip and she promised to write. To my astonishment, she did. One day, about six months after my departure, she must have settled down with a dictionary and a few biros of different colours – all on the point of expiring – and wrote to me. I could imagine the trouble she'd had finding the writing-pad, and saw her setting it squarely on the oil-cloth of the kitchen table before she braced herself and sat down.

'Dear Billy – Thank you for all them lovely post cards of all them lovely places . . . ' (the second 'them' was scored out and she substituted 'the') ' . . . the lovely places your boat goes to. I hope you are feeling well and not getting sick with all that forn food they . . . ' (clearly, that didn't look right. The word 'forn' was scored out provisionally while she turned to the dictionary for the spelling of 'foreign'. She looked it up under 'forn', though, and ran into all those variations on 'fornication'. 'Hah,' I imagined her chuckling with disbelief, 'this dictionary's got a wan track mind! An' the word A want's no' in it.' She resumed the letter, leaving 'forn' as an option for the reader which wasn't quite right but couldn't be proved wrong) ' . . . its nice that you miss my cooking. Its very quiet in the house now that its empty that Mr Mulvenny is away as well. This is because I was . . . ' (the word was so effectively scored out that I couldn't read it) ' . . . I was stupid to get into some bother with the polis and Mr Mulvenny moved to Andys house.

57

Maybe its best because there are no stairs and he can get into the garden. On Sunday there Andy came down for a visit to let me see the baby and he says Mr Mulvenny likes the change. Hope you are all right. Yours sincerely, Isa Mulvenny.'

On the face of it, that seemed to me good news. With Mr Mulvenny out of the way perhaps she would recover some of her old ebullience, and drop as many cups as she had a mind to. And she could go back to work. I was sure her old employers would be delighted to have the services of an assistant so popular with the customers. I wrote urging her to apply and suggesting, too, that she should take in another lodger. 'But,' I warned her, 'ask him first if he likes the smell of camphor. Nowadays I can scarcely get to sleep without it.'

As I sat writing in the oven that was my cabin on the Gulf, the pungent smell did come vividly back to me and at once it seemed that an idyllic existence could be enjoyed at the Mulvennys' in cool, rainy Greenock. In fact, whenever I thought of my three months off when this long trip was over, I saw myself, rapturously drenched, climbing the hills above the town. So when my first trip was over I did not go home immediately. I went to Greenock and I hired a car because I had a plan – a surprise. My car at the close-mouth excited the interest of neighbours and before I'd reached the first landing I knew all the facts about Isa's 'bother' with the police. It was a charge of 'drunk and disorderly' – a common enough charge on that street, but more scandal than Andrew could bear. It upset him particularly since Andy had to come down from the City to bail her out. It happened the day after I left. The sudden panic of being alone in the house with that man drove her out on the street to spend my going-away present. On the day I came back, that incident – and a great deal more – had gone from her mind. I'd sent her a note, of course, to tell her I'd be dropping by. It gave me an odd feeling to stand in front of so familiar a door, and to knock.

'Hello, Mrs Mulvenny!'

'Good afternoon, Billy. Come in. It's nice to see you

again.' The greeting was cool, and very carefully enunciated. I crossed the threshold with some unease. 'Just go right through. You know the way.'

'Were you just going out?'

She seemed taken aback. 'No. Not immediately, no. If you clear away those books you'll find a place to sit down.'

'Do you have another lodger?'

Now she was offended. 'Lodger! No, I have not.'

'I wondered who was reading all the books,' I laughed.

'I am reading them,' she replied severely.

'Oh!'

'I was expecting you off the next train but . . .'

I broke in excitedly, 'Well, you see I came by car and . . .'

Her voice went right on, mechanically, '. . . I've got the tea things ready. Excuse me.' She turned and walked out of the room, repeating those words in exactly the same tone, 'I've got the tea things. I've got the tea things ready. Excuse me.'

It was as though she had rehearsed exactly those words and no others, but doubted if the information would carry conviction to a second person. And she was quite changed. She'd let her hair grow again, and it was plaited and coiled, just as it used to be. And dyed very near the colour it used to be. She wore her 'costume' – the same matching jacket and skirt – which had not been cleaned but had been pressed under a damp cloth so often that the material now hung unnaturally rigid on her much thinner body. I looked around. The house had a prematurely abandoned air. All the ornaments had been cleared away and there were bags and packages and parcels stacked against the wall – ready for departure. For a moment I thought she'd guessed that I planned to take her on the first holiday of her life. Or maybe she wanted me to take her away from that dingy street, for good.

The rattle of the tea tray approached and she came in, carrying it very high. 'I'm sorry there's not much to eat, but you won't be staying long, will you?'

'I don't want anything to eat, thank you.' I reached in my bag. 'And I've brought you something to drink.'

'Something to drink?' she asked, frostily.

'Yes. Look. Whisky! I thought we'd have a little celebration.'

'Just put it back in your bag, please. You know I don't approve of strong drink, especially at this time of day. What if somebody should come in?'

'Who?'

'Here's your tea.'

I was dismayed by how she sounded and her manner. It was as though I was talking to a woman I'd never met before. Still, I had an ace that would bring back all the old warmth and affection. 'Mrs Mulvenny! How would you like to come home with me for a holiday? To my parents' house. I've told them to expect you and I've got the car outside. We could go now. Right away!'

Then, I swear, she stared at me exactly as she'd stared at me when I brought news of Andrew's accident. The words I'd used then and now seemed to connect. 'Go now!' she repeated. 'Car waiting. Is he hurt bad?'

'What?' I asked, and tried to rouse her to the present. 'Mrs Mulvenny! Will you come with me for a holiday?'

She rose and retreated to the position she'd held when I arrived. And the mechanical words came out again. 'I'm sorry there's not much to eat, but you won't be staying long, will you?' Or maybe she was just ashamed that she couldn't prepare a full meal for me. I took a sip of tea and then I tried again.

'As you know, we live in Sussex. You'd like it there. I've got three months until I start my next trip. I could take you round all the places and you could visit my . . .'

'No.'

'Why not?'

'Well, as you see, I'm ready to move. To Andy's house. Any day now. Any day now. It would never do if he came to collect me and I was away for a holiday.'

'I see. I'm sorry. I didn't know you were going to move.'

'You surely didn't think I'd stay in this empty house on my own?'

'No, of course not. I'm sorry. I didn't know the . . . situation.'

'Why should you? I mean, it's not as if you were one of the family. Everything's quite different now. Quite different.'

'Yes.'

'More tea?'

'No, thank you. I, er . . . brought you this, too.' From my bag I took a small, flat package.

'What is it?'

'Open it and see.'

'Tell me what it is, please.' The absurd notion occurred to me that she feared it might be an odd, very flat, bottle of liquor.

'Just a little present from Hong Kong. A silk scarf. Turquoise.'

She took the package. 'Thank you. That's a nice word.'

' "Turquoise"? It's a bluish-green colour.'

'Yes,' she said. 'Turquoise. That's a *very* nice word.'

There was nothing else for me to do but go. She saw me to the door but closed it before I'd taken one step down. When I reached the half-landing I looked back. But no, the door was closed. My shoes clacked loud on each of those stone steps and I noted that whoever's turn it was for the stairs must have declared open-roster. It wasn't surprising. Many of the front doors I passed on the way down were covered by sealing sheets of corrugated iron, heavily sprayed with graffiti. I got into the hired car and set out for England, and Sussex and – undeniable now – home.

That was the last I heard of the Mulvennys for a long time. Isa was right. Why should I think of myself as one of the family? Perhaps I had interfered too much. The changes and the progress of the Mulvenny family were really not any of my business now. And there was my own life to consider as, year by year, I edged up the promotion scale. Still, I kept Isa up to date with itinerary sheets and occasionally I sent postcards to her at Andy's house. But she never wrote to me again.

When I'd qualified for all the necessary endorsements to my Chief's Ticket, I applied to become an Engineering

Surveyor ashore with Det Norske Veritas. One of my early postings was Clydebank, on the other side of the river from Greenock. I was reluctant to cross over even to visit my former home. When I did it was to discover that the old street was deserted. Most of the close-mouths were bricked up and a lot of the windows were boarded over. It didn't seem worth while getting out of the taxi to trudge around a demolition site. The whole town was so depressing that I kept away from Greenock for the next two years. Only when I had the comfort of a confirmed posting to London did I go back across the Clyde. It was a rainy night and to brace myself for a farewell tour of the familiar places I went into a dockside pub. The air was thick with smoke and packed to the door. I ordered a double whisky and, while I waited for it, my ears became tuned to some variety in the cacophony of sounds which surrounded me. In particular I detected the sound of a piano being played. When I got my drink I started bull-dozing my way in the direction of a yet unseen pianist, who was playing 'The Rose of Tralee'. When I saw him I knew him instantly. 'Joe. Joe Harper!'

'Yessir, that's me. An' if ye want a tune it'll cost ye a drink.'

'I've brought you a drink.'

He didn't look up. 'Put it where I can see it. Whit dae ye fancy?'

I shouted to make myself heard above the clamour. 'Just play "The Rose of Tralee".'

He squinted up at me pugnaciously. 'Whit sa gemm, Jimmy? That's wha-a-am playin'.' But he stopped playing and craned round to look at me more closely. 'Dae A know you?' he shouted.

'Or "Down Mexico Way",' I suggested.

'Fur God's sake, make up yer mind. Wan drink, wan tune.'

'We met at the Mulvennys'.'

'Mulvennys?' Then he gave the top of the piano an open handed slap. 'Aye! Ye mind me o' . . . You were the boy.'

'Why don't you take your drink over here. It's quieter.'

He poured the drains of the drink he'd been drinking into the drink I'd bought for myself and followed me to a less noisy corner. When we were seated he inspected me more closely and nodded. 'You were the boy – the ludger they had – afore she went daft.'

'What?'

'Daft! Mad, ye know. Stupit wumman! Hiv ye seen her?'

'I saw her just before she moved away, to her son's house.'

He gave the table a thump, but made sure he was holding the glass with his other hand. 'Christ Almighty! Are you daft as well? Moved?' He shook his head vehemently. 'She hasnae moved. She's still there in that rat-hole o' a tenement. They'll knock it flat roon aboot her.'

'No!'

'Oh, but aye! She's no right in the heid, I'm tellin' ye. Never has been since the "champeen runner" dumped her for his fancy son. And that's twelve year ago.'

I felt a stabbing pain of guilt in my chest. 'She's still there! Are you sure?'

'Certainly, I'm sure. Ella goes up noo an' then. She says the place is thick wi' muck and maist o' the furniture's been broken up for the fire. But Isa's still got all her belongins packed and ready tae move.' He tilted his chair back on two legs and gave a scornful grunt. 'Huh!' He lurched forward again, thrusting his finger at me across the table. 'Where could they move her? And who'd have her?' I didn't answer him. I couldn't wait a moment longer, but I heard him calling after me as I fought my way out of the bar, 'Hey! Hey, wait a minute. How's about another drink?'

I ran all the way. I ran along street after rain-slicked street, through deep puddles around blocked drains and over broken paving. As I got nearer, the street lights which still worked were fewer, but I knew my way. Solitary pedestrians backed against the walls in suspicion or fear at the sound of my pounding footsteps, and cursed me as soon as what they'd thought was a danger had passed. And all the time my feeling of guilt was tightening with the tightness of my breath. Finally, I staggered up to the close and stopped to gasp for a while before I climbed the stairs.

I knocked loudly on the door and waited. There was no reply. I knocked again, even louder. The echo of the sound came drumming back and filled the stairwell. When that had faded, I thought I heard a faint scratching behind the door. I glanced up at the fanlight and convinced myself there was a dim glow. Then I heard the voice, soft and hopeful. 'Andy? Is that you, Andy?'

She opened the door slowly, edging it open, and I slapped my hand to my mouth to muffle the exclamation, 'Oh, God!'

Her hair was white and it hung, disordered, in long greasy strands round her face. And – at last – she was 'not so tall'. She was stooped and leaning heavily on the door-handle as she peered out from the dim lobby to the comparative brightness of the landing. If I was not Andy, she had no idea who I was.

'I'm a friend of Andy's,' I said.

'Aw, that's nice. It was him A wis expectin', but you come in anyway.' Her voice, though broken and distant, had resumed her old accent and a ghost of its former warmth. 'In ye come an' sit doon for a minute.'

There were no chairs; just a few wooden boxes. 'It's all right. I'll stand,' I told her.

'What does Andy say?'

I had the answer to that implacably fixed in my mind. 'He's coming to see you tomorrow morning.' I did not add that the promise would be kept if I had to drag Andy bodily to that room.

'Tut, tut, tut,' she shook her head, apparently at her own foolishness in forgetting. 'It's tomorrow it is. I've got everything ready, y'see, but I couldnae mind exactly . . . when.' She smiled, and again – for a moment – I saw the person I'd known through the distressing mask of what she had become. 'D'you work in Andy's office, Mr, er . . . ?' she asked sociably.

'Yes.'

'That's nice.'

'Mrs Mulvenny, are you cold?'

'Naw. It's rainin', is it no'? It cannae be very cold if it's rainin'. Damp, though. Sometimes I feel the dampness.' But she brushed that aside. 'Tomorrow. You tell Andy I'll be ready – as early as he likes.'

'I certainly will.'

She sat on one of the boxes and rehearsed the scene. 'I'll put on my costume and I'll sort my hair . . . and I'll wear that lovely scarf he gave me.'

'Scarf?'

She took on her old exaggerated pose of incredulity. 'Did I not show you that?' she exclaimed and pushed herself to her feet with vigour. She knew precisely where to find it in the piles of cartons and packages and brought it to me. 'There! Still in the box.' The box still had the ornate label of the Hong Kong gift shop. She took out the scarf and draped it over her arm. 'Finest silk, that. Andy gave me it for my birthday. And a lovely shade. It's what they call "turquoise".'

Next morning I was on Andy's doorstep at seven o'clock. I waited in the tiled hallway until he got dressed. The most prominent piece of furniture there was a long table burdened with silver trophies. Everything Mr Mulvenny had ever won, and sold, had been reclaimed or refashioned. In the centre was the Levi-Allen Shield – and it bore only Andrew's name. Andrew himself I glimpsed as we were leaving. He was alone in the dining-room eating breakfast, impeccably dressed as ever and not looking a day older than the last time I'd seen him. He glanced up as we passed the open door. Obviously, he did not recognise me but was in the habit of acknowledging Andy's business associates.

To be quite fair to Andy – or as fair as it's possible for me to be – he did not hesitate in coming back to Greenock with me and he was obviously shocked when he saw his mother. Nor did he raise any objection when I insisted that I should be consulted about a suitable nursing home. Evidently his neglect of it had made his business my business, too. It would have been wrong to keep her in his house for I knew, and he realised, that nothing would drive her further from sanity than having to live with her husband once more.

When a suitable place had been found and regular visits arranged Isa seemed willing enough to move in. I arranged with the Matron, in confidence, that regular reports of her health and progress were to be sent to me at our London headquarters. The following week I left for a five year posting. Once there I sent her occasional gifts and greetings cards. At first, she thought they were from that assistant in Andy's office. Eventually, she knew they were from me; and knew who I had been. That small gain cheered me a lot.

There is a soft double tap on the door of the sleeping compartment and the attendant thrusts himself in, tray first.

'Good mornin', sir. Here's your tea. I'll just put on the . . . Is there anything wrong, sir?'

'No, no. It's just the light makes my eyes water.'

'We'll be in in half an hour.'

'Can I still get a connection to Greenock from Central?'

'Platform eleven. It's electric now. Do ye know Greenock?'

'Aye, very well. Or what it used to be, anyway.'

'Hasnae changed much,' said the attendant, rather grimly. 'You're going home, then?'

'No. I'm going to a funeral.'

The cemetery is exposed to a strong, rain-laden wind blowing up from the Clyde. I check with the gate-man and find the plot before anyone else arrives. And when they come they aren't many. I stand some distance away and watch the ceremony. When it is over, I walk away. There is nobody I want to talk to. It is Andy who runs after me, calling, 'Bill? Bill Thompson!' I turn to face him and see that Mr Mulvenny, too, is wheeling himself towards me.

'Hello, Andy.'

'Hello.' He catches at the arm of the wheel-chair. 'Dad, you remember Billy Thompson?'

'Yes, indeed I do,' says Andrew. He is perfectly composed. 'Will you come home with us, Mr Thompson, and have some refreshment?'

'No, thank you. I'm going straight back to London.'

'I was sure it was you,' Andy says. 'How did you hear about it?'

'From the Matron at the nursing home.'

Andrew nods. 'Ah, yes. A very officious lady. She's put

66

you to a great deal of trouble. Maybe she thought you were a relative.'

'I know you were fond of my mother,' says Andy. 'And it was very good of you to make the journey. You're sure you won't come back with us?'

'Quite sure. But what a pity you didn't invite *her*, before it was too late.'

Andrew's bright eyes don't flicker. 'Mr Thompson, I think we've got to face it – the woman was no use to herself.' The chair wheels skid on the gravel as he returns to those who think that is true.

A Friend of Dosser Farr

Like all closed societies, the world of engineering has its own initiation ceremony. Before he is fully admitted, the apprentice has to be 'greased'. What horrified me was *where* he had to be greased. In the shipyard where I served my time, there was an adamant preference for the genitals. Since I'd come directly from a minor English public school, that should not have surprised me. And, given the mechanical parallels of piston-rod and regulator-valve, it might even have seemed apt. Nevertheless, I was determined that nobody was going to do *that* to *me*. Thinking of it now, the whole business is fairly amusing, but then, when I was seventeen the prospect of such abject humiliation was terrifying. For a few months I was successful in avoiding any group of my fellows which wore that menacing collective smirk and as I got used to the place I persuaded myself that they'd forgotten I hadn't been 'done'. I'd reckoned without the lack of supervision when, during roof repairs, we had to work on the night-shift.

Bent at my lathe in the Light Machine Shop, I realised that Frank, my only reliable friend, was smiling over my head.

I looked around but could see nothing unusual. 'What is it?'

'Nothin'!' But he smiled even more broadly.

The distraction was fatal to the gunmetal valve I was turning. The tool dug under the centre-line and the whole piece rocketed out of the chuck, smashed the machine-lamp and fell with a denouncing clang in the sump. I fished it out and revealed the deep gash in the valve face.

'What shall I do?'

'Whi' everybody else does,' said Frank, unperturbed. 'Dump it in the Dock Burn an' steal another yin fae the store.'

'I'd better wrap it up in something.'

'Wait tae ye finish the shift. The wey you're gaun, there's likely tae be mair.' But again, he was looking behind me and this time I turned quickly enough to see the advance of four or five older apprentices – one of them carrying a large can of axle-tallow.

Frank said, 'Ye cannae dodge it this time, Billy. Ye're gonnae get greased.'

'I won't let them.'

'Ye cannae stop them.'

'Will you help me?'

'Naw. But I'll no' help them.'

The long gallery of the machine shop was lit only by the individual machine lights and, since the light on mine had just been shattered, the area around me was practically dark. Frank, who had undergone the business with perfect composure more than six months before, moved away. I gripped the damaged valve tight in my hand and waited. I heard Jock Turnbull's deep laugh and I turned to face that way, but immediately I heard from the opposite direction the creak of the long footboard as someone stepped from the concrete floor onto it. Then they were all on top of me. My wrist was caught and banged against the tail-stock so that the valve again dropped loudly in the sump. I struggled as hard as I could – trying to wrestle my way *under* the machine. They gripped my legs and pulled me back on the footboard. Staring up I saw the repair tarpaulin on the roof flapping against the dark sky before faces and shoulders and arms blotted that out. And I could smell the sickly, thick tallow. My head was pulled up by the hair so that they could start stripping off the one-piece suit of dungarees under which I was wearing shirt and trousers. Between their legs I caught a glimpse of the labourer, Lord Sweat-rag, moving sedately towards us. Suddenly I stopped struggling and was immediately commended. 'That's it, son,' said one voice. 'Lie back an' enjoy it!' said another. They were so intent in getting the dungarees off, they had stopped holding *me*. When they'd dragged the overalls down to my waist somebody undid my belt. I wriggled free; under the machine and up the other side. The apprentice who was fielding there reached out to grab me but Lord Sweatrag – as though unaware of what he was doing – blocked the tackle and I slipped away. I ran the whole length of the machine bay towards the foreman's box, then out onto the dockside. The foreman had had his feet up reading the paper but stirred himself to see me disappearing towards the river.

They did not pursue me immediately. Probably because such a concerted movement would have brought the foreman out of his box. I edged my way into a nest of empty oil drums, then lay back to recover my breath. The sky was overcast and everything was quiet. Only gradually did I become aware of the river lapping in the disused dock. This was the Dock Burn that Frank had mentioned where, traditionally, apprentice mistakes were consigned to the not-so-deep. I also realised why the greasers hadn't bothered to pursue me. This short stretch of dock was completely blocked at each end. The only way out was through the door by which I had escaped. They could come out and get me any time they felt like it. Tonight, they would not give up. With a stabbing pain of fear in my stomach I tried to think of how I could possibly escape the trap. If they came out, the pile of oil drums would be the first place they'd look. I started moving away from them, sliding my back along the wall.

My progress was blocked by an upright steel girder set into the wall. Looking up I discovered it was the support for an old loading gantry which jutted out, like a fixed crane, high over the dock. It was a feature I had not noticed, even in daylight; my pursuers would never think of it in the dim spillage of light from the lamps on the far corners of the building. I started to climb the warped and rusted access ladder which rasped at my fingers as I pulled myself higher. My arms were aching when I reached the top platform of the gantry and a position clear of the dockside, high over the water. For some irrational reason I felt safe there, but I also began to feel cold. It was now after eleven o'clock on a raw October night and I didn't even have the protection of my dungarees. There was no sign of the greasers. All they had to do was wait in the warm for my inevitable return.

About an hour later, when my misery had increased to such an extent that I felt like drowning myself to teach *them* a lesson, I saw – however incredibly – a boat directly below me. It was a small rowing boat; and there was a man in it – fishing! 'Hello,' I called softly. He reacted as though God had called softly. He jerked round and fell on his back, almost swamping his craft. 'It's all right,' I said, but that didn't seem to reassure him. He blessed himself with a pale, urgent hand. When he realised it was neither God nor the angel of death perched above, he rowed into the dockside and I climbed down to talk to him.

'Can you get me out of here?'

'That depends. Who the hell are ye?' He had a light little voice with a strong Irish accent.

'I'm an apprentice. There are people after me.'

'The polis?'

'No,' I said, and at once realised I should have said yes. 'Who are you?'

'James Farr,' he said proudly. 'But they call me "Dosser" Farr.'

'Mr Farr, may I come into the boat? I want to get clear of the shipyard. Now! Do you know how to do that?'

'Of course I know. We get out the way I got in. Under the wire when the tide is low. Put your foot there, lad, and I'll hold steady.'

I lowered myself into the dinghy and Dosser started pulling for the dock entrance and its insecure barrier. Evidently the tide wasn't quite low enough. The jagged ends of the wire tore my shirt as we scraped under. It seemed Dosser knew his way around those backwaters and he soon beached the boat at the rear of a disused factory. Then we began a long trail through back streets.

There were two men on the demolition site of a ruined tenement. The old man – a night watchman – sat at his brazier against a wall. The young, smartly dressed man stood staring into the fuming charcoal. Neither of them seemed surprised when Dosser squeezed through the protecting fence but the old man's expression changed when I quickly followed.

'Peter, my friend,' called my guide, 'I have brought you this young visitor.'

'And ye can take him right back,' his friend replied.

Dosser's finger tips pinched my elbow. 'The man doesn't mean it,' he murmured, leading me towards the warmth.

'A mean it, Dosser. It's bad enough puttin' up wi' you, never mind yer waifs an' strays.'

'He is neither waif nor stray — *and* he is not wanted by the polis!'

'Huh!' the watchman grunted at the novelty of this.

My rescuer went extravagantly on. 'No! His name is Bill Thompson and he's a refugee from persecution that I plucked from the very dockside not half an hour ago. He was perched upon a girder and he's cold.'

'Get in there at the fire,' said the younger man.

I moved closer to the brazier.

'So, I told him to jump down into me boat . . .'

'Is that right, son?' asked the watchman.

'Yes. I was hiding on the dock and I saw Mr Farr fishing.'

'Fishin', b'God! Where wis this?'

'The Dock Burn.'

'Ah!' He nodded with satisfaction and turned to Dosser. 'And whi' did ye catch this time?'

'Enough to make it worth me while,' announced the wizened little man. He undid his long ragged coat and from its many deep interior pockets produced a gleaming haul of gunmetal valves, small brass flanges and white-metal facings.

The watchman was impressed. 'Things are lookin' up, eh?'

'Oh, they are surely,' Dosser agreed. 'As apprentice quality in that place is going down, I'm glad to say.'

I laughed. 'If you'd waited you could have had one of mine.'

The scrap-fisherman was alert to my potential. He beckoned me to sit down beside him. 'So! Are ye on the brass-work, then? I have a great interest in the non-ferrous range; whether it's made into anything or not. I mean, why should you go to the bother of working on a piece, scrapping it and throwing it in the Burn where I have to trawl for it – when ye could jist give me it?'

'Don't listen tae him, son, or ye *will* be wantit' by the polis.'

Dosser was offended. 'Am I not tryin' to save that shipyard money.'

'*Save* them money?'

'Certainly – on labour costs.' The young man laughed and Dosser, nodding at the appreciation, went on, 'They have to pay these boys, y'know, for the *time* they spend on the work they scrap.' He turned earnestly to me. 'You see that, don'cha, Billy?'

I nodded. The steady glow of the brazier had restored a lot of my self-confidence and at this secluded encampment in the middle of the night, my real initiation – into adoptive Scottishness – began.

'Where are ye from, son?' the young man asked me.

Before I could answer, Dosser leaned protectively in front of me and whispered, 'He's English!' His tone suggested the sympathetic acknowledgement of a rather messy disease.

'We *know* he's English,' Peter retorted. 'We kin *hear* that. But where in England?'

'I don't see that matters a bit,' said Dosser huffily.

'Sussex,' I revealed. 'On the coast. A town called Lancing.'

'And whi' made ye prefer Greenock?'

'Now, don't embarrass the lad. Here! I've brought ye some soup.' Dosser produced a can from yet another pocket.

'Did ye pull that outa' the Dock Burn as well?'

'I did not! I stole it from a very clean grocery.'

'Is there anything you don't steal, Dosser?' his host wondered as he opened the can and poured the soup into a blackened pot.

'Certainly. I don't steal what I can't steal. And what I can't steal – I can do without.'

While Dosser took off and *folded* his ragged coat, the old man made further enquiries. 'Sussex, eh? And where are ye livin' here?'

'I'm lodging with a family called Mulvenny.'

'No' Andrew Mulvenny?'

'Yes.'

'The runner!'

'Yes. Do you know him?'

'Know *of* 'im. An' his picture's always in the local paper – winnin' somethin'. So! He's takin' in ludgers, is he?'

'Only me.'

The man snorted. 'Oh, a good quality, right enough. But still, it's no' quite the thing fur a gaffer.'

The young man spoke to me. 'So, you're in the Light Machine Shop, eh?'

'Yes. At the moment. I shall be moving about, though, getting experience in different departments.'

'Sure. More of a *visitor* than a real apprentice.'

Peter said, 'This is my son, Michael.'

'Your son, Michael, of course,' Dosser exclaimed. 'I thought his name was Martin.'

'No, Michael,' the son insisted.

Dosser advanced with an extravagant flourish of his hand. 'I'm glad to see you again. I'm a great friend of your father's. And your mother's, too. Oh, yes, Maisie knows me well.'

'I've heard her mention you.'

'Michael, eh?' Dosser stroked his chin as though aware he was being conned but good-naturedly willing to play along. 'Back from the sea for a while, Peter says. Going to give the old town another chance. Settle down?'

'No. Just a short break. I'm going back on Wednesday.'

'Going back!'

'Yeah. Signing on again at Southampton first thing on Thursday morning.'

'Of course,' murmured Dosser the world-traveller, 'signing on. Again. For how long would that be?'

74

'Well, on the tankers that's another three years, at least. I've been standing-by for Chief – and the chance has come up.'

' "Standing by",' Dosser repeated. He loved such knowing expressions and hoarded them. 'But you could get an engineering job ashore, could you not?'

'Easy!' said the young man's father, but did not raise his head.

'Aye!' Michael retorted with a vehemence which implied that this was a standing argument between them.

'Easy enough,' the old man repeated.

'As what, though? I'm damned if I'll go back to the tools. The only place to get promotion is in the South.'

'Things'll change,' said Peter.

Dosser mediated. 'Oh, surely! Things are changin'.'

'Not in this place.' Michael moved away from further argument and encountered me. 'Scotland's for the hard graft, eh boy?' He turned to the others to offer proof. 'That's why they sent him up here to learn his trade. But you can be damned sure they don't expect *him* to stay here.' He looked down at me. 'Do they?'

'No.'

'No! You'll go back South.'

'Ah!' Dosser sighed. 'But for him, poor lad, that's just going home. It's a different thing altogether for you, Martin. You are home.'

'Michael!'

'Whatever you say.'

It was exactly there in the conversation that for the first time I felt a sudden distancing of myself from where I was actually sitting. As they went on talking it seemed I was looking down at them. It happened several times while Michael was there.

Peter adopted a reasonable, disinterested tone through which I sensed hurt and disappointment. 'We thought, when ye did decide to come ashore, ye'd settle here. You did say as much.'

'That was in a letter. Now I've seen it again, things are different. Aye, now I've seen it – and *smelt* it again! The air's thick wi' dampness and rot.'

75

'Lately, the weather's been wet.'

'Huh! If the weather was all!' Michael moved away to pace the perimeter of the lighted space, so that he seemed to be moving against a circular void. 'It's a feeling. Like a clammy hand on your chest that ye have to push against every step ye take. It's always tryin' to push ye back where ye came from. And that hand is the hand in the glove of every bugger ye meet. They're all at it. Anxious. Holdin' back. Pressin' down. Makin' sure that you're still in the grip.' He paused and threw back his head in a bitter laugh. 'On Saturday, there, a man stopped me in the street. He'd read in the papers they were demolishin' this place. He wanted to know . . . Holy God! He wanted tae know what street we were *hopin'* tae move intae. Yeah! Though we left this dump twenty years ago, though I've been round the world seven or eight times, though I didn't even know the bastard's name – he was worried in case we might get one up on him.'

'Did he say his name?'

'He thought I *knew* his name!'

'What did he look like?'

'He looked like a frightened wee man whose only chance of keepin' his place is to keep everybody else back.'

'Oh, I know the sort well,' said Dosser. 'They're usually Special Constables, too.' The others laughed. 'Or at the very least, paid informers.'

Again I was watching them from a distance, but now from a different angle. Michael shivered. 'Well,' he told his father, 'now you've got better company I'll away home to bed.'

I saw him gather up his coat and start to move out of the lighted area.

Dosser called after him, 'Will I be seeing you again . . . Michael?'

'I don't think so. Unless you're here on Wednesday.'

'He'll be here,' Peter said. 'He's here every night. Cannae get rid o' the bugger.'

'Okay.' Michael waved and squeezed out through the fence.

When he'd gone I realised that I was drowsing quite close

to the brazier and the talk was not nearly as clear as it had been.

Peter was saying, 'He'll drive down overnight on Wednesday.'

'Is that so?' Dosser marvelled. 'I suppose he knows the way to England all right?'

'He's done it often enough.'

'I doubt if I could manage it at all.' He took out his mouth-organ and blew a few exploratory chords. 'To any particular place, I mean. No, no. That is another country altogether.'

'He jist has tae stick tae the road.'

'Of course, there will be only one road going, and none at all coming back.'

Peter seemed to agree with that, for I did not hear him answer as Dosser played 'There's A New Moon Over My Shoulder'.

What with the hot soup and the fire and Dosser playing his mouth-organ and Peter Duncan reciting at length from the works of Robert Service, between dozing and listening, I spent a very enjoyable night at the demolition site. It was after five o'clock in the morning when I wandered back to my digs. Wearing an enormous unclaimed duffle-coat that Peter had lent me I strolled through the sleeping town. It worried me that Martin . . . I mean, Michael – Dosser's confusion began to confuse me. I wondered why Michael was so bitter. He was a fully trained engineer; as I hoped to be. But not here. The outrage of the attempted greasing had convinced me that I must get out of Scotland and away from the barbarous training that my father had imposed on me. I knew it was no good writing home asking him to reconsider and to send money for my return trip. I must get home in person and decline to be sent back. Nothing was worth the humiliation and fear I'd gone through that night. I must simply run away. When I reached my digs I waited in the street until the blind was raised on the kitchen window then went up to bed. It was with some difficulty that I was wakened to hear reports that I'd been drowned. And I was delighted.

The apprentices had kept guard, waiting in vain to

complete the greasing. At daylight they searched the narrow stretch of dockside, found nothing and told the foreman. He recalled my panic the last time I was seen. In the plating-shop, Mr Mulvenny was informed and he came straight home to wake me.

Naturally, I took advantage of the situation and recalled that I had indeed *almost* drowned but was sucked out of the Dock Burn by the tide and cast ashore outside the yard. This story preserved Dosser's fishing trips and, more importantly, put the fear of God in the greasers. *And* I got the rest of the week off work – to recover. Little did they guess that I would not come back at all. If only I'd started hitching my way south that night I could have had them dragging the Dock Burn for my body. The very thought of that revenge cheered me. And I had thought of how I would escape. Michael was driving South on Wednesday. I would simply go with him.

In the afternoon, as soon as I thought everyone would be back at work, I was out and down the hill to see if I could find either Michael or his father at the enchanted ruin where I'd found shelter. The demolition team was going full blast, forcing monstrous entry upon tiny rooms. The variety and colours of their wall-paper seemed absurd, yet oddly touching; probably because the decoration which should only be seen indoors was now thrown open to the sky. So, the people who had put it there to adorn their lives were rudely made vulnerable, without their permission.

As I passed the filthy window of a small stand-up snack-bar, I caught sight of Dosser and went in to talk to him.

'Mr Thompson, again!' He bowed, flourishing a thick sandwich.

'Do you live near here, Mr Farr?'

'I live in two places, only,' he said. 'On me feet and on me back. That's the extent of my social position. Let others make a mark on the world – I'll jist make a dent in a dry tarpaulin.'

'And where is your tarpaulin?'

'Nearby. I prefer to be near one of my investments.' He nodded proprietorially across the street to the demolition site. 'That old tenement, now, is bulgin' wi' non-ferrous materials. When that was built there was none of yer plastic rubbish for pipes and fittings. No! It was lead, solid copper and brass from top to bottom. And it's worth a damn sight more this day than the day it was new.' He sighed. 'The very best of stuff.'

Both of us peered through the steamed-up window as though a quinquereme of Nineveh had just berthed by the far pavement.

'I suppose that's why they need a night-watchman,' I said.

'Just so. But the night-watchman likes company.' He gave me a consciously sly smile and wink, by which I understood that there was no duplicity. Peter Duncan knew why Dosser was always hanging about. And Dosser knew that he knew.

'But you've known Mr Duncan a long time, haven't you?'

'Indeed I have! Since he used to live there.' He leaned closer, allowing me an intimate close-up of the sauce dribble on his stubbled chin, and whispered, 'That man is keepin' watch on his own ruin.'

'What did he work at before he retired?'

'He did no work a long time before he retired. When he did work, though, he was a tool-maker. Till his hand got unsteady through drink.'

I was impressed. 'Tool-makers earn a lot of money.'

'Oh, they do that. And he spent even more. A terrible waste.'

'His son seems to have done very well.'

Dosser nodded vehemently as he emptied the remnants on his plate into the palm of his hand. 'That's Maisie's doin'. Mrs Duncan. She's the little woman held everything together when there was nothin' to hold. And she's workin' still.' He applied the loaded palm to his mouth with a gesture which could have been mistaken for covering a languid yawn. 'Now!' he said, 'you can oblige *me* with some information.'

But the Duncans were still nagging at my attention. 'I suppose they really don't want Michael to go away.'

'They do not. In fact, havin' their son home to stay is what they've been countin' on for the rest of their lives. Maisie, anyway. Havin' him in the town, a successful man, would have made everything worth it, d'ye see?'

I nodded. 'You mean, she could stop working?'

'No,' said Dosser. 'That's not what I mean at all.' And he had no intention of enlightening me. He went on, 'You were sayin' the metal store, in that yard of yours, runs right back to the river.'

'No. I didn't say that.'

'Did you not?' He was all alert surprise. 'Well, somebody told me that's where it was.'

'No, it's beside the gate-house; so they can unload from the street.'

He slapped the counter. 'Ach, to be sure! And how often would that be . . . they unload the material?'

'I don't know.'

'I could make it worth your while.'

I laughed at him. 'I really don't know!'

'You could find out, though.'

'Yes.' I did not tell him that there was now no possibility of my gaining any further information about the shipyard.

'And would ya do that for me, Billy?'

'Why do you want to know?'

He put his arm round my shoulder. 'I'm thinkin' of retiring, d'y'see, and nothin' would suit me better than to make off wi' a full bloody lorry-load of gunmetal forgings.'

'Can you drive?'

'Drive what?'

'A lorry. Can you drive a lorry?'

He brushed this aside. 'Well, I've never *drove* a lorry, if that's what you mean. Or anything else, for that matter. But there can't be much to it. Look at them ignorant yobbos that's to be seen in lorries day and daily. You don't think they could do it before they did it, do ya?' I stared at him incredulously and he took my silence as a proof of his point. 'Not at all. Drivin' the thing's the least part of it – if I only knew *which* lorry; and when.'

'Will you have another sandwich?'

His weathered little face folded into a delighted smile as

he misinterpreted the offer. 'I will.' He patted my arm. 'It's a pleasure doin' business with you, Billy.'

'But . . . ' I protested.

'I know! But don't you worry about that side of it. I have a friend with a little furnace that could soon melt a lorry-load – and the lorry as well, if we're pushed.'

Leaving Dosser in the snack-bar, I walked across the street and peered through the fence just to make sure that the magical space we'd occupied around the brazier was still there. Everything looked quite different. I stared around me wondering if this was the same site. I walked hesitantly beside the fence, then stopped and looked up at a jutting piece of what had been a second-floor flat. For no visible reason, but instantly, I was reassured.

On Wednesday morning I sorted out what few possessions I could take with me and still give the impression that I was only going to be away for the week-end. Nothing and nobody was going to stop me. Late in the evening, carrying a small bag, I went down the hill to the site. I got through the fence but was shy of emerging too suddenly into the light since only Michael and his father were there and they were talking amiably together.

Michael moved the bench nearer the brazier. 'Are the kids still goin' out as guizers?'

'Sure,' his father said. 'Battalions o' them.'

'I wouldn't have thought there were many kids left in this part.'

'Not now. But I've seen the day.'

'Oh, aye!' Michael smiled at the recollection. 'It was great fun.'

'Aye,' Peter sighed, 'I remember when you use'tae go oot for ye're Hallowe'en.'

'Always as a pirate wi' the . . .'

'Naw! Pirate? Naw, I remember the wee face wi' the . . . white . . . and big eyes. A mask. An *elf* or somethin' it was.'

Michael looked at his father briefly with pained perplexity then insisted, 'I was the pirate, always the pirate. The elf was Martin.'

'Oh!' said Peter and nodded quickly. 'But was he old enough tae go oot on Hallowe'en?'

'Well, if I was old enough he was old enough.'

'Aye, I suppose so,' the old man laughed uneasily. 'But I never think o' you two bein' twins.'

'I do.'

'Still?'

'Still.'

'I'm surprised you remember him clear at all. Martin died before you were . . .'

'I know well enough when he died. And why.' There was a callousness in his voice he hadn't intended and he watched anxiously as his father abruptly stood up, faced away, then started swinging his arms, as though to repel a sudden chill. 'Are ye cold?' the son asked.

'No. It's jist the change. The heat'll soon build up.' He turned back again to face the brazier. 'There's more warmth here in the open than we ever had in that house.'

'Maybe because you don't have to pay for the coal.'

Peter leapt from sadness to anger. 'What! It was me tae blame, ye mean?'

'No, I just meant that . . .'

'If we'd had the money I'd have kept him warm. An' well fed. If I'd been in work we could've moved fae this damp hole. But it wisnae jist lack o' warmth. Holy God! I would have burned the whole bloody street if it could have kept him alive.' He stared wildly at his surviving son who hunched deeper in the coat.

'Sure,' Michael grunted.

'There were families better placed than me that lost children in times like that.'

'I know.'

'We did everything we could for that boy. But he was frail. No' like you. Delicate. No' a bit like you.'

'No. I was always a sturdy bugger. Luckily.'

'You should be thankful for it, instead o' . . .'

'I'm thankful. But I wish there'd only been one of us.'

'You?'

'Or him. But one. And it would've been cheaper.'

'That's a rotten thing tae say?'

'I hate like hell to feel there's a gap at my side.'

'A gap?'

'When I'm away it's a gap. Whenever I come back here, though, it's more than that. Martin's beside me, or watchin' me. I wish to Christ I knew what he *expects*!'

For me, hidden in the shadow, that strange distancing again occurred. I was looking down on the two men. But now I knew beyond any doubt that what I'd been aware of above and around that place was Martin. I felt it had been with his eyes I'd watched them before I knew of his existence.

'What d'ye mean, expects?' Peter asked.

'I've been trying to think if I ever made him a promise.' The young man glanced, almost apologetically, at his father. 'When we were weans, y'know – maybe I promised him somethin' and . . . I didnae do it.'

'Weans make a lot o' promises.'

'But did he ever say anything aboot that? Can you remember?'

'Aboot you?'

'Aye.'

The old man thought for a few moments, anxious to be of use in this odd – it seemed to him pointless – conversation. 'He was awful fond o' you.'

Michael gave a sob that carried intimately across the whole clearing. 'Oh, my good Christ, I know that!'

Suddenly I felt ashamed to be eavesdropping upon them and, to suggest that I was arriving now, I rattled the fence then walked boldy towards them.

'Hello, Mr Duncan. I've brought back your coat.'

He took it absent-mindedly. 'Thanks, son.'

Michael was quicker to regain his composure. 'Well, er . . . Billy, you're all dressed up tonight, eh?'

'Yes.'

'Where have you been?'

'No – I'm *going*.'

'At this time! Where?'

'If you don't mind, I'd like you to give me a lift home.'

'Ye're not afraid o' the dark are ye?'

'No,' I said, then struggled to work out why he'd ask that.

'He means home, tae England,' Peter guessed.

'If you're going to Southampton I can get a bus from there, home.'

'Sure,' Michael said. 'But I'm not leavin' right away.'

'No. I'd like to wait here until you're ready.'

'Are your people expectin' ye?' Peter wanted to know.

I shook my head. 'No. I've been given a few days off work and I thought I'd spend the time at home. It'll be a pleasant surprise.'

'It will,' the old man said. 'A son that wants to come home is a pleasant surprise all right.'

'Oh, God!' Michael groaned under his breath.

From the darkness, a cracked but still lyrical tenor voice sang, '"Trumpeter, What are you sounding now?"' Dosser advanced upon us. He carried two bulging carrier bags. 'I tell you,' he said, 'I've had a busy day of it.'

'What's that ye've got?'

'Provisions!' the thief replied and started unpacking various groceries and fancy-goods that he'd stolen for the event. 'Seein' as how Martin will be drivin' a fair distance, I have brought various kinds of sustenance.'

'A'm payin' ye nothing for any of that,' Peter warned him.

'Would I expect payment?' Dosser invited our derision.

'Yes!' said his friend.

'No payment. Jist a wee favour, maybe.' He turned to Michael. 'Since ye've got yer car out there, I wondered if you'd learn me to drive before ye go.'

'But I'm going *tonight*,' Michael protested.

'I know that. Sure it's tonight I mean.' Dosser gave me – his fellow conspirator – a mock-despairing look that people could be so obtuse.

'Dosser, there's no time for that.'

The little man was hurt. 'Oh?' He looked around him for signs of activity. 'What's goin' on then? What am I missin' that's takin' up all your time?'

'I mean, it would take you longer than that,' Michael said.

'Why? D'ye think I'm stupid?'

'Mr Farr, it takes months to learn to drive,' I said.

84

'Can you drive?' he challenged me.

'No. But I'm saving up for a car. I'm too young to drive yet.'

'Exactly. Too young to know anything about it.' He turned magnanimously to the others. 'Still, never mind me. We can make a night of it anyhow.' He made a comprehensive gesture at the loot piled by his feet. 'What we can't use I'll take back tomorrow for a refund.'

'Don't be daft!' Peter told him. 'This has all been stolen.'

'Of course it has. That's the work in it. The refund is a bonus.' He explained to Michael, who might not know his system, 'I never steal money, y'see, but there are times when I do need ready cash.'

'I see.'

'That's what these women's blouses and girdles and what-not are for – takin' back.'

'What!'

'Shops are used to that.' He sighed, sharing the resignation of shopkeepers. 'Sure, if women don't know their *own* sizes why should I?'

'Aren't they suspicious in the women's department?' I asked.

He shook his head. 'They think I have a very fussy bedridden wife, or that myself is one o' them funny fellas.'

'But what about the receipts?' Michael asked.

Dosser gave him a patient smile. 'What makes ye think I can't steal them as well? I have a whole selection of receipt-books, and quite a few date-stamps, too. Oh, yes. I'm a great believer in havin' things legal.'

We all poked about among the bric-a-brac, food and fancy-goods that Dosser had provided. Peter put aside the bottles, the biscuits and the meat-pies. Dosser himself made sure that his items for return were safely repacked. Michael selected chocolates and a small pack of thin cigars for the journey. That left me with two packs of bunting and a few crepe-paper lanterns; with which, presumably, Dosser had intended decorating the demolition-site. While the men were drinking I did my best to add this seasonal touch to the lighted space. I strung out the bunting between the posts on the drying-green which had lain behind the tenement but was now a desert of rubble. Where the strings crossed I hung paper lanterns. Michael helped me in this absurd decoration of his former home.

'I don't know what the foreman's goin' tae say in the mornin',' he said.

'He can say what he likes,' I replied, thinking of my own foreman. 'We'll be away and out of reach.'

'Funny, we never thought o' doin' this when we lived here.'

Beyond the space of the drying-green, I could just make out a small, ruined, stone structure. I asked Michael, 'Why does that coal cellar have chimneys?'

He laughed. 'That's not a coal cellar. That's the wash-house.'

'Out there!'

'Where else? Each of the families in this close would have the use of it one day in the week. That was the day we had soup for breakfast, dinner and tea.'

'Why?'

'My mother had no time tae make anything else. Wash-day was a major operation and she was out here from morning till night. We helped her.'

'Martin and you?' I gulped, thinking I'd trapped myself by knowing about Martin. But if I had, Michael didn't notice.

He smiled. 'We could just manage tae carry an empty bucket between us – or a clothes-peg bag on our own.'

'Did you stay off school?'

'This was before we were old enough for school. Martin loved gatherin' up the clothes-pegs. He saw them as wee wooden horsemen ridin' the clothes line in single-file.'

I couldn't imagine it, but then, probably, I had never seen the right clothes-pegs. 'Like soldiers?'

'Aye. Then, when the washin' was done we'd all have our bath in the boiler.

I was amazed. 'In a boiler?'

'Sure. It was a big wide copper tub surrounded wi' concrete and wi' a fire under it. Martin and me used tae love that. 'B'God, it was big enough for us tae *swim* in. All that warm, sappley water!'

'And was the fire still going, under it?'

'No, no. Your mother let the fire out as soon as the whites were boiled.'

'And the whole family used it, one after another?'

He nodded. 'Good hot water was hard tae come by in those days. But when ye came out of there ye warenae just clean, ye were bleached!'

His face was illuminated by an orange glow as he tried to make a lantern hang straight. He was smiling and I realised that far from resenting the conditions in which he'd once lived, he remembered them with affection. As we picked our way back to the circle of light around the brazier I marvelled at the image of those two little boys *swimming* in a copper cauldron. We rested a while, then Dosser brought out his mouth-organ and played a few songs to which only Peter seemed to know the words.

Before long, it was time for Michael to go. 'Are you ready for the off, Billy?' he asked me.

'Yes, whenever you like.'

Dosser protested, 'Must ye go, Martin? So soon!' The words seemed to bear more weight than he could have intended.

Michael stared at him almost angrily for a moment, was about to correct the name again, but instead asked, 'Did you know my brother, Martin?'

'Your brother? I didn't know ye had a brother.'

'You mean, you didn't know Martin had a brother.'

Dosser was confused. 'That must be it,' he said, doubtfully.

Michael persisted, 'You remember Martin?'

'Oh, surely! As a tiny sliver of a boy. He used to follow me around. Always wanted to help.'

Peter, seeing his son's distress, tried to dismiss the subject. 'You're all mixed up, Dosser. Forget it!'

'Mixed up I may be, but I'm not likely to forget your lad. Nor will he forget me. Didn't he tell everyone he met, in his wee piping voice, "I'm a friend of Dosser Farr"!'

Michael sat down abruptly, as though pulled down.

'Are ye goin' or not?' his father asked him.

'Sure. Sure! I'm going.' He pushed himself to his feet again and I waited politely at the fence as the men shook hands. 'I'll be *back*,' Michael promised.

'Visitin',' Peter said blankly.

'Aye.'

Dosser, the experienced driver, added some advice. 'Watch yer speed, now. And keep to the signs!'

Walking towards me, Michael laughed and called back, 'What signs?'

Martin's friend was less sure of specifics. 'Whatever signs there are. Dangers and warning. There's more than you on the road; even through the night.'

'I'll let you know how I get on,' Michael called and waved to the two men standing by the glowing brazier. Again the duality intervened. I saw me at his side as he waved and looked down on the heads of Dosser and Peter from above and behind them.

As we drove through Greenock and on into Port Glasgow, the headlights shone on several roving bands of 'guizers', all aged between five and twelve and many of them wearing full beards as part of their elaborate costume. They trudged along in businesslike fashion from one housing scheme to another, like a greatly increased band of Snow White's dwarfs. 'Were you never out as a guizer?' Michael asked me.

'No. We don't do much for Hallowe'en,' I said. 'But this is the time we were all preparing for Bonfire Night.'

'That's right. It's Guy Fox night you hold.'

'Maybe that's where you get the name "guizer".'

Michael chuckled. ' "Guizer Fox"? No. I think it's more from "disguise".'

I wanted him to tell me about Martin and so – although I knew the answer – I asked him, 'What were you disguised as?'

'A pirate. And the water always got under the eye-patch when I dooked for apples. Always ended up wi' a soggy eye-patch.'

This was incomprehensible. 'Water?'

'What else would ye dook in?'

'That depends on what dook *is*.'

'It means, "ducking". Ducking for the apples, floating in the water.'

Evidently he thought he'd made the whole bizarre ritual quite clear and I didn't want to test his patience with such outstanding questions as – what water, and how did the apples get in the water, and why must they be removed without using your hands? We drove on in silence up the bank of the Clyde towards Renfrew, before skirting the south of Glasgow to join the A74 at Hamilton. The flashing beacons which mark the deep channel of the river traced a dotted line over the black surface of the water curving far ahead of us. Before we'd cleared the other side of the city I was asleep in the car – but, somehow, awake at the demolition site. Through the presence there of Martin I saw and heard all that occurred, or dreamt that I did.

Peter – as so often in his earlier days – was drowning his sense of loss in whisky. Dosser, too, had given up a fishing trip for that evening. They were excellent company for each other; one providing sentimental music and the other dramatic recitation.

The most effective of these was 'The Shooting of Dan McGrew' and for his audience of one – doubling as the kid that handled the music-box – Peter spared nothing in recreating the atmosphere of that hectic night in the Malamute Saloon. They were resting on the glow of a fine performance when they were unexpectedly joined by the woman who was known as Maisie. Peter's wife. She was a small, thin woman who – even over rough ground – moved with quick decisive steps. Her lips were pressed firmly together giving a stoic, though rather sad, expression to her lined face. She looked older than her husband; and probably felt it.

'What the hell are *you* daein' here?' he asked.

'Hello, Maisie!' Dosser greeted her. 'You just missed "The Shooting of Dan McGrew".'

"Oh, A heard it. A heard it. I was jist pickin' ma wey across the shincut, there, when two guns blazed in the dark.'

'Did you duck?'

'Damn nae fear o' it! They guns hiv been blazin' in the dark ever since A kin remember.'

Peter was annoyed. 'What are ye *here* for, Missus?'

'Because I'm fed up wi' weans chappin' the door. Ye don't get a minute's peace.'

'Ye could put oot the light an' kid-on ye're no' in.'

'The hoose is empty enough withoot sittin' in the dark. Especially th'night, efter he left. But it's they weans . . . they keep chappin' anyway – tae find *out* if ye're no' in. And look through the letter box.' From under her coat she produced a bundle wrapped in a shopping bag that she'd been keeping warm against her stomach. 'So I boiled these spuds in case ye were hungry. Is the can on?'

Dosser rose in courtly fashion to receive the offering. 'You're a thoughtful woman, Maisie. And a few boiled spuds is about the only thing we're short of.'

Her husband was not so easily won. He said, 'You'd better get back or you'll miss the last bus.'

'I came on the last bus,' replied Maisie.

'This is a work-place, no' a bloody home-fae-home.'

'Oh? Ye're forgettin' it wis ma home, long enough. We knew and liked mair people here than we ever met again.'

'Bloody nonsense,' Peter growled.

She ignored the interruption. 'Ye know, comin' in that bus A wis used tae, and risin' tae get aff at the same old stop made me feel ower twenty years younger.'

'Is that a fact?' said Peter with heavy sarcasm. 'And what dae ye think of it, noo ye are home?'

Maisie surveyed the wide, desolate gap among the ruins. 'They must have took back the furniture – *again*,' she said, tartly. 'I'd recognise this anywhere.'

'D'ye want a drink?' Peter asked, avoiding well-contested ground.

'Where did ye get drink?' The question packed accusation and disapproval in equal measure.

'Oh, it's just a wee something I stole,' Dosser modestly confessed. 'For Martin's goin' away.'

'He means, Michael,' said Peter wearily.

'I should think so.' Maisie drew her coat tightly around her. 'For Martin's been away a long while.'

90

Dosser shook his head dubiously and murmured as though to himself, 'Not away from here, surely.'

Peter tried the same diversion again. 'Well, Missus, dae ye want a drink or no'?'

'I thought it was Dosser's bottle,' she countered.

'Holy God! All right. Wid ye take a drink if *he* asked ye?'

'I would not!' She turned to the drowsy gift-bringer. 'Thanks all the same, Dosser.' But she did sit down. 'So, Michael got away all right?'

Peter nodded, 'Oh, he got away. He got away fast.' He pushed the poker into the depths of the charcoal and jerked it upward, causing a flare of sparks. 'Did ye lock the door?'

'What's there tae steal?' the woman scoffed.

'Did you?'

'I locked the door! D'ye want the key?'

'Whit wid A dae wi' the key?'

'Lose it!'

Dosser had now divided the potatoes in three portions and was preparing to serve them on pieces of wrapping paper. 'Did ye bring any salt?' he asked.

Maisie reached into a pocket of her coat and produced a screwed up corner of a brown paper bag. 'There ye are. But don't give *him* much. It's bad for his heart.'

'You leave ma heart tae me,' said Peter.

'That's where it's always been,' his wife retorted. She could not resist scoring points against him; whether or not they were deserved, or even apt. Her whole attitude seemed bent on levelling an enormous score that her husband had unfairly gained many years before. Now, whatever he did, he could only lose. Apparently Peter understood this and offered only token resistance.

Maisie glanced around to find that Dosser was asleep. Then she looked beyond her husband to the black outline of the ruined tenement. 'They havenae far tae go now,' she said. 'Is that Mrs Chalmers' close they're at?'

'Naw, further up. They'll be at number thirty-seven the morra.'

'Miss Nisbit!'

'Aye.'

'Widnae surprise me if she comes round tae see they dae it right!'

'They know whit they're doin'.'

'And what'll you be doin', when they're finished?'

'Nothin'.'

'Oh, I thought ye might be lookin' for anither job as a watchman.'

'Maybe.'

'Suits you fine, doesn't it? Out all night – just like your younger days.'

'Whit the hell wis there tae stay in for?'

'Ye could have taken pleasure in your home.'

'I wis tellin' Michael, it's warmer here now than it was then.'

'We could have made it cheery,' said Maisie grimly.

'Aye, we could have. If you could have changed. Back tae whit ye were before ye lost that boy.'

'Me? I lost him! If you'd spent more . . .'

'When Martin died the life went out o' you!' Peter's voice overrode her protest. He was sure of his ground because she had confessed as much before now. 'Since then ye've put a cold hand on every chance we might have had. Maybe that's why Michael skinned out.'

'That's got nothing tae dae wi' me!'

'It has!' Peter gained strength from her defensive tone. 'He mentioned that – the cold hand.'

'That's a lie! Oh, you'd say anything tae shift the blame.'

'Is it a lie that you blame me? That the kiddie died? And at every turn since then ye've done everything tae make sure I'd never forget it. Or that Michael would never forget it and that's why . . .'

'Peter! No.' The oddness of Maisie calling him by his first name quite deflated Peter. He stared at her and she went on, 'That's not what I blame ye for. If there's blame for that it *is* mine. For that, I blame only myself.'

'But it spreads out, woman. It spreads out over me. Over the three of us. And you've no right to blame yourself at all.'

'It's no' somethin' I'd claim as a right,' said Maisie softly.

Peter, finding his opponent so quickly vulnerable, was at

a loss and added with surprising gentleness, 'That's not what I meant.'

'I know. Ye say more than ye mean. Always have.'

'What I meant was that Michael feels guilty aboot Martin. That's how he had tae get away.'

'How can that be?'

'He thinks Martin's holdin' him responsible, or somethin'. He cannae get it oot his system that he's failed Martin over the years.'

'We a' fail somehow, over the years,' Maisie was prepared to confess.

'And the older ye get, the mair ye regret it,' said Peter. His wife knew this was the nearest he could come to an apology and, for the moment, she was content.

They were interrupted by the sound of drumming and I woke in the car driving south. We'd run into a rain storm at Abington. It grew heavier as we climbed towards Beattock Summit. The windscreen-wiper on my side swept maddeningly from side to side without *touching* the windscreen at all. Michael offered to stop and try to fix it but I told him not to bother. 'There's nothing to see, anyway.'

'We'll stop for something to eat at the border,' he said. 'I'll have a go at it then.'

'When do you think you'll get to Southampton?'

'Six or seven o'clock.'

'And when do you have to sign on?'

'I don't *have* to sign on. It's a matter of choice.'

'Oh, I thought they were expecting you.'

'No, no. It's just that I know what ships are crewing-up.'

'So, nobody's employing you at the moment?'

'Nobody's employing me till I sign on for the trip.'

'I don't think I'd like not being sure.'

'It gives ye freedom.'

'When I qualify I'm going to have a long-term contract.'

'Quite right. You'll be just the kind o' man the owners want, long term. In fact, I think you'll be the kind of seagoing engineer they'll want to keep ashore.'

I laughed. 'Does that mean a good engineer or a bad one?'

'It means, a man wi' good connections in the front

office – that happens tae be an engineer. Great for impressin' the customers.'

'Do you think I could do that?'

'Certain. They'll be your kind o' people.'

I thought that what had started as a compliment was deteriorating into rather snide and unfair carping. 'What do you mean, my kind of people?'

'Oh, people you'd like.'

'I like Dosser Farr.'

'He's good for a laugh.'

'No, as a friend. Is that the sort of person I'd be dealing with?'

'Hardly! There are very few people like Dosser hiring oil-tankers.'

'Just as well, or they'd be scuttled for scrap.'

'Aye,' Michael laughed. 'Or run aground. Dosser wid want ye tae run it aground tae collect the scrap.'

'And he'd only take the "non-ferrous", at that!'

As we drove between the forests of Ae and O'er it seemed as though the car was attempting to part an unbroken curtain of water.

Shouting above the demented drumming on the roof, I suggested, 'Maybe you should stop until it eases off a bit.'

'If I stop we might start floatin',' Michael shouted back. He crouched over the wheel, lips parted, teeth clamped tight, as he tried to pick out what lay ahead of us. All I could see was a constantly shifting barrage of needle-pointed lights as our headlamp beams were flung back at us. The pounding of the rain had buckled the wiper arm on my side and it lay twitching across the bonnet. Perhaps, if Michael had stopped to fix it before we ran into the worst of the storm, the accident could have been avoided.

It happened at the roundabout south of Lockerbie. A truck loaded with steel rods was immediately ahead of us and as it moved onto the roundabout, Michael cautiously followed – assuming that the truck would take the main exit. He could not see that it was turning more sharply at an earlier exit to the left. It was as though a steel spear was suddenly thrown between Michael and me. The weight of shattered windscreen dumped in my lap made me twist

94

round and I saw the look of stupefied wonder on Michael's face. There, not more than six inches from his eyes, hung a white elfin mask. It hung from the longest rod protruding over the tail-gate of the truck. It had been tied there as one would tie a piece of rag, to mark the length of the load. On this particular night, though, the driver had light-heartedly substituted a Hallowe'en mask.

Obviously the truck-driver had no idea what had happened behind him and, finding his way clear, he continued off to the left. The steel rod was drawn from our windscreen with a rasping sound and the mask dropped, grinning, on top of the instrument panel. Michael could not take his eyes off it. Of course he had been shocked by the collision, but now I realised that his shock was deepening when the danger was over. To him it must have seemed that he'd been forcibly stopped by Martin. That mask at which he was staring was identical to the one in which his twin brother always went disguised at Hallowe'en. I dared not say anything. We waited what seemed a long time, with traffic moving past us in the downpour.

Fatigue and shock made my head swim. I stared at the mask and it seemed to recede from me. Then, through the curtain of gleaming rain, I thought I saw the tenement. It was that same jutting corner of the second floor flat I'd noted, but now a small white face peered hopefully over the jagged edge of bricks. The image was soon blurred by the spray from the passing truck. Yet it lasted long enough to bestow on me the same curious afflatus I'd felt, looking up at the real building.

Gradually Michael eased his frozen posture and began to sob as though gusts of breath were forcing their way out of him against his will. And the rain was now pouring through the gaping windscreen. At last, my companion spared me the trouble of deciding what we should do. He'd made up his mind what *he* must do. Slowly, he jerked ahead on the roundabout. He swung past the exit to the south, then the exit to the west. With the mask staring at him from blank wide eyes, he completed the full circle and headed back from where we had come. I remembered Dosser's voice. Signs . . . Dangers and warnings, he'd said . . . there are more on the road than you. Michael could not lightly deny the most potent sign he'd ever been given. Nor, really, did he want to.

When we got back to the demolition site – soaked, cold and starving – it was almost daylight. Peter must have been off completing his round before the end of his shift for, at first, we could see only Mrs Duncan. She was dozing huddled in her husband's coat. The brazier was almost out because there was no point in refuelling it. As we drew closer, Dosser rose from the ground behind her, stretching himself.

'Ah, Michael!' he said. 'Did ye forget something?'

'No,' said Michael, 'I've changed my mind.'

Maisie shook herself awake. 'What was that?' She half rose from the bench then, fully appreciating that it was really Michael who stood there, slumped back on the bench.

'I said, I've changed my mind.'

'What happened to your suit?' his mother asked.

Michael shrugged. 'We got caught in a shower.'

'Dosser, get some more coke on that fire! They're soaked through.' He scuttled to obey and Maisie, with considerable self-control, remarked to her son, 'Yer father'll be pleased you're back.'

'And you?'

'Depends. Are ye home for good?'

'Yes.'

'I'm pleased,' said Maisie.

Michael nodded. 'Good.' He looked around at the debris of the night watch. 'Is there any whisky left in that bottle? We need something for the chill.'

'Surely!' his mother said. She lifted the bottle. 'I think I could go a wee nip, masel. Quick, before your Da finishes his round.' But she wasn't quick enough. Peter walked into the clearing as the three of us were downing a jolt. He advanced slowly, keeping his eyes on Michael, determined not to give anything away. Maisie reassured him. 'Michael's decided to stay.'

'That's good news.' Then his voice leapt out of all

restrictions. 'That's bloody good news.' He suddenly grabbed Maisie and whirled her round.

'Peter! Don't be silly!'

'I'll be silly if I feel like it. An' I've never felt mair like it.' Still holding her, he swayed happily from side to side and sang, '"After the ball is over, After the break of day . . ." '

Dosser immediately took up the tune on his mouth-organ and as Michael and I dried ourselves at the revived brazier, Peter waltzed Maisie around us. They scuffed through discarded paper wrapping, over the powdered mortar and fragments of brick. Maisie began to enjoy the dance and she sang too.

Michael, while still smiling at them, turned to me. 'I'm sorry ye didnae get home for your Hallowe'en.'

I confessed. 'I wasn't just going for Hallowe'en. I was running away.'

'Were you?' he said, as though it didn't surprise him. 'That made two of us.'

'Yes. But you were running away from home. I was running back to it.'

'Aye.' He nodded but he was not really interested in what I was doing, or why and I wondered if, now, the gap at his side would close; if his being home 'for good' was what Martin expected of him. Quite involuntarily, but aloud, I said, 'Yes!' He jerked his head round to face me, as though I had answered exactly the question he'd been asking himself at that moment. The sound of his parents singing, the scuffing of their feet and the plaintive, reedy sound of Dosser's mouth-organ wrapped around us. Michael stared into the revitalised brazier then, very deliberately, pulled from his pocket the mask and dropped it onto the glowing coals.

When I went back to work there were no further attempts at greasing. Apparently it had been decided that anyone who was recklessly prone to suicide would just have to do without lubrication round the genitals. But they made it plain they were disappointed in me. That lasted until I was about to depart from 'the shops' into the drawing office.

That's when the axle-tallow caught up with me. And it was from the drawing office that I caught up with the Duncans.

On one of my infrequent visits down the shops I met Michael Duncan working there. He'd been appointed to lead the Works engine-test team. It was a highly technical position requiring a great deal of experience. Michael was quite evidently enjoying the job.

'I know what I'm doing,' he said. 'And the money's good. On top of that there's the odd "jolly" as guest of Gebrüder Sulzer in Switzerland.'

The diesels we built were Sulzer design, manufactured under licence from the Swiss company. I smiled. 'Very nice! How are Gebrüder Sulzer?'

'Flourishing.'

'And how are your parents?'

'My mother's fine, but my father died a couple of years ago.'

'I'm sorry.'

Michael shrugged. 'His heart. He wasnae up to all that night-watchin'.'

I nodded sympathetically but I was thinking that 'night-watching' was a very imaginative expression. 'Do you ever see Dosser Farr?' I asked him.

'Occasionally.'

'I wonder if he ever learned to drive.'

'Drive?' Michael stared at me blankly. Obviously he'd forgotten about that. It may have been that he had purposefully put out of his mind all the events of the night we both tried to escape into England, but more likely he was the same as others I met who, perversely it seemed, forgot exactly the things I'd chosen to remember.

'I'd better get back to the office,' I said, suddenly aware that perhaps Michael couldn't remember who *I* was.

As for Dosser, he certainly postponed his retirement. For a long time after that he continued to hang around the yard gates, no doubt logging the time and nature of deliveries to the metal store. Occasionally, I saw him in shops disdainfully fingering the most unlikely items of merchandise. He nodded civilly enough but I could tell that he was disappointed in me, too. Clearly it was my loss that I had not gone into business partnership with him. Anyone so lacking in enterprise as that deserved to work for a living.

Store Quarter

Some people are 'car' people, whether they can afford a car or not. They are those who are not charmed by their fellow men in the mass, in the crush, or in the queue. They can be seen, sitting or swaying in public transport, fervently pretending they are alone. And I've always been one of them although I did not realise it until I left school, home and England at sixteen. Deprived of the parent-chauffeur service, I immediately began to save up to buy a car of my own. On my wages as a Clydeside apprentice that took some time and, while I saved, the weekly trip from Greenock to Glasgow Tech. was done by train. It was possible to be alone on the journey *to* the college, but coming back there were always some of my classmates.

'Hey, Billy!'

I didn't respond and held the tutorial notes firmly in front of me as a barrier. The four of us occupied the four window seats in the 'empty' I'd chased at Glasgow Central. Strictly speaking, they had invaded *my* compartment.

Archie Hemple was not to be ignored. He shouted to the youth sitting opposite me, 'Pull that bloody book aff 'im, Deanie.' This was done and I immediately turned to stare at my reflection in the dark window. Archie tried again. 'Hey, Billy!'

'Yes?'

'Is it right, you're gonnae buy a car?'

'Yes.'

'Whi' kinna car?' asked the note-snatcher, throwing the book back in my lap; thus scattering all the loose sheets of graph-paper.

'An A35. A Baby Austin.'

'That's awful *wee*. A wee Austin'll hardly haud the four o' us!'

'It will hold *me*,' I announced firmly.

'An' its only got *two doors*. I hate gettin' oot tae let somebody else in.'

'True enough,' Archie Hemple agreed with Deanie. 'Ye'll hiv' tae get somethin' bigger than that. Look at the length a' ma legs!' And he showed us one of them by stretching it into the crotch of the quiet little boy who sat opposite him.

'Get ye're fuckin' feet aff me!' said the quiet little boy and big Archie did so – immediately.

'Oh, helluva sorry!' Archie saved face with effusive apology.

'A'd've thought,' Deanie told me, 'your old man wis rich enough tae buy ye somethin' *com*fortable.'

'His old man rich?' asked Archie.

Deanie gave an effete wave of his hand and imitated my accent. 'Can you not tell? Oh dear, yes!' Then resuming his own voice reported, 'Consultin' engineer. Heid o' a big firm, an' that. Makes a packet, dis'nae, Billy?'

'Christ! An' a' he's layin' oot fur is a pokey wee Austin?'

'My father has nothing to do with it. I'm buying the car for myself.'

'When are ye gettin' it?' the quiet boy asked. I tried to remember his name. It was Tommy or Terry or something.

'March.'

'Next month, eh?' He seemed to consider this with more care than it warranted. 'Hiv ye paid the deposit?'

'No. I'm buying it outright. It's cheaper that way.'

He nodded with what looked like worried approval, but Archie was less acute. 'Don't be daft! How can it be cheaper tae pay the full price when you could put doon a third o' that an' still get it?' He appealed to the quiet boy for common sense. 'Use the heid, Tony!'

'He means he'll no' hiv tae pay the interest,' said Tony.

Both Archie and Deanie were amazed, but it was Deanie who expressed their offended credulity. 'You mean, you've actually saved up the *whole* amount?'

'Yes.'

'An' ye've got that ready tae lay doon?'

'Yes.'

'An' ye never though'a the never-never as soon as ye had enough fur a deposit?'

'At that time I wasn't old enough to sit the driving test.'

Archie thought some retribution was in order. 'Well, A hope ye get landit wi' a clapped oot banger that bloody well explodes on ye.'

This puzzled me for a moment before I was able to inform them. 'I'm not buying a second-hand car. I'm buying a new one.'

Their astonishment turned to deep irritation, if not anger, and they held silence until we reached Port Glasgow where both Archie and Deanie got off. Not for the first time I was made aware of a crucial difference between my upbringing and theirs when it came to the use of money. We use it like soap. They use it like water.

Tony and I were alone in the compartment for the remainder of the journey into Greenock. Because he was so small and compact, with a pinched, sharp little face, he gave the impression of being much younger than the others. But he must have been at least the same age as me, and probably a good deal wiser. He put aside whatever was worrying him and – though I'd never talked to him before – seemed willing to be friendly.

'They clowns,' he said, shaking his head, 'they've nae idea.'

'About money?'

'Aboot anything!'

'Do you work in the yard?'

'No' in your yard. Further up. In Lamonts.'

'Oh.' They were small ship-repairers and their workers therefore lacked the kudos of new-building. Tony apparently read my reaction and gave a bitter little grin.

'It's no' everybody can buy everything new,' he said. 'Is this a college course you're on?'

'It will be after my third year.'

'Aye, A thought ye must be wan o' the college boys.'

'After my third year,' I insisted.

'Sure. But ye know it's there waitin' fur ye, don't ye?'

'Yes. If I pass everything before then.'

'You'll pass all right,' he assured me bleakly. 'You were reared tae pass.'

'I failed my driving test first time,' I offered.

But that was not enough to grant us equality. 'Ye can take that as often as ye can afford it, though.' The train slowed and he looked wearily out at the first of the platform lights. He got up. 'See ye next Friday,' he said, 'if no' before.'

'Yes. Good night!'

As it happened, I saw him the very next evening. The Fol De Rols were doing their season at the King's Theatre in Glasgow and I went there for the first house. He was sitting in the middle of an evidently well-fortified coach-party. They were led in every rowdy response by a fat middle-aged woman with an enormous bust and an equally outsized hair-pad supporting what was then the fashionable coiffure. Her constant rocking and tossing with laughter had shaken the pad well off-centre and must soon dislodge it altogether. I mentioned this distraction to Tony when I met him in the foyer during the interval.

'I've been spending more time watching that than watching the stage.'

'Ye're jist as well,' he said glumly.

'Don't you like the show?'

'It's all right. But it's always the same.'

'Pity you had to get stuck in the middle of that awful coach-party.'

'Aye.'

'Look! There she is now. She must have done some repairs.'

'Who?'

'That fat, vulgar woman with the hair-piece. She must be looking for the . . .'

'She's lookin' fur me,' said Tony. 'That's ma mother.'

His mother came towards us and now that she was on her feet I noted that her feet were crammed into delicate little shoes with absurdly high heels. She seemed to be tethered like a balloon between the fine tension points of her top-knot and her toes. It was difficult to see how she was able to remain upright.

'Here, Tony!' she called as she approached. 'Whit did ye dae wi' the bliddy raffle-tickets?' He started searching in his pockets but she did not await their discovery. 'Who's this?' she wanted to know.

'A mate o' mine fae the Tech. He's no' wi' us.'

She examined me. 'I should think no'! Be a while before *he's* in the club. Eh, son?' She gave me a playful dig in the stomach and laughed.

'Here's the tickets,' said Tony.

She snatched the book from him while still looking at me and asked, 'Wid' ye like tae buy a few? It's in a good cause.'

'Twenty percent commission, she means.'

She turned to her son. 'How'd ye like me tae shove these doon your throat, smart-arse?' she enquired.

'He disnae want tae buy any,' Tony unblinkingly insisted.

'Suit yersel'!' Her attention moved in the direction of the bar. 'Surely tae God somebody's got me a drink b'noo.' And she crunched off to find out, continuing to address Tony without looking back. 'Ask the boy if he wants tae come on the bus!'

'Dae ye?' he asked me. 'Ye'll get a free run back if ye like.'

'Yes. Thank you,' I lied. It was a small sacrifice to make for my mortifying clanger. 'Does your mother run a lot of these outings?'

'She runs every bloody thing she can get intae.'

'It must be very tiring for her.'

His chuckle remained entirely within his chest. 'Tiring?'

'Yes. Unless she's very fond of people.'

'You're no'?'

'Not in groups.'

'Don't care fur them much masel',' he said. 'In groups or otherwise.'

'Then why did you come?'

'She gets them tae hire me – as a kinda steward.'

'Oh! Do you enjoy it?'

'It's a' right, tae somebody vomits on yer suit. She claims them fur that as well, of course. An' runs the raffle on commission. Oh, aye. If there's a back-hander gaun, naebody can beat Big Delia.'

'Oh! Is that your . . . ?'

'Ye've heard'ae'er!'

'Yes, I've heard my landlady mention her.'

'She in the Store?'

'Pardon?' Even after two years I had moments of difficulty with the foreign language of industrial Scotland.

'Is your landlady a member of the Co-op?'

'I don't know.'

Again he was looking at me in that worried, rather furtive, way. Then he seemed to reassure himself. 'Anyway, I expect she'll hiv' her ain number.'

'I'll ask her,' I said, since he thought it a matter of such importance.

'Y'see, ma mother deals in the Store for people that hivnae got their ain numbers.'

'Like . . . buying wholesale?' I hazarded.

'Only fur weddins,' Tony murmured, giving no inkling that this was a joke. He saw my confusion and smiled. 'You don't understan' this at a', dae ye?'

'No,' I said. Also, I saw no reason to try and understand it. 'I think I'll go in now,' I said. I'd seen Big Delia returning, drink in hand. She stopped me.

'Here, son! We've got a spare seat if ye want tae sit beside Tony.'

'No, thank you. I'm fine where I am.'

'But ye're all on yer own. That's no' right. Fine lookin' young fella like you.' She winked at me then turned briskly to her son. 'Ye'd better start gettin' them oot the bar an' intae the right *row*.'

'They'll no' move tae the bell rings.'

'So, next time bring a bliddy bell wi' ye – an' ring it.'

Tony laughed and his mother threw her free arm around his neck. 'Away ye go an' tell them the bell rang while they were havin' a piss.'

'But whi' if they've no' . . .'

'Christ, son, they've a' had a *piss*. If they hivnae, the

bliddy stage'll be *floatin'* before the end.' Tony moved off to relay this information and his mother called after him, 'But if the aulder wans hivnae been, make sure they go.'

'I think I'll move in now,' I repeated.

'I'll come in wi' ye,' Delia said. 'Somebody has tae be there tae catch the buggers comin' doon the stair.'

I was desperately aware of people looking at us as – on her insistence – we marched arm-in-arm back to the auditorium.

'Whi' *is* your name, son?'

'Bill Thompson.'

She squeezed my arm. 'A'm awful glad Tony's found a pal. He's been such a solitary boy.'

'Perhaps he prefers his own company.'

'Aye, but ye know where that leads,' she said cryptically.

As it turned out, that journey back in the bus was not a *minor* sacrifice. Given the choice again, I'd prefer crucifixion. As we set off the noise was incredible. Each member of the coach-party was either singing or shouting at somebody who was singing. Every now and then they changed about and apparently there was no *one* song that any *two* people wanted to sing, or hear. Meanwhile, those who could still lurch were lurching up and down between the seats and across the seats. Either way, they had to squeeze round Big Delia – who was everywhere. Adding impetus to this mêlée was the coach driver who decided to dispense entirely with first gear and attempted racing starts whenever he'd been stopped by lights or heavy traffic.

But such a prodigious output of energy could not be sustained and by the time our kangaroo progress reached Erskine it was possible to hear yourself speak. The person who spoke to me, when Tony thrust her down beside me, was a beautiful dark-haired girl. She had a slow, demure smile and abruptly pushed her thigh against mine.

'This is nice, isn't it?' she said, ostensibly referring to the coach run.

'Yes.'

She reached across to unfold my arms and take my hand.

'I don't always come in the bus,' she remarked, or

106

warned – it was difficult to tell which meaning she intended, for her body seemed to have a mind of its own.

'I never do,' I told her. 'Oh! I'm sorry, I'm sitting on your hand.'

'That's all right. If ye just open your legs a bit.'

'Ah! . . . Yes.' I laughed. 'These seats are a tight fit.'

'I'll bet everything's a tight fit for you.'

'Pardon?'

'A mean, ye're a big fella. An' gettin' bigger . . .'

'What?'

' . . . I expect.'

I coughed as though I was just clearing my throat. 'The Fol De Rols are a favourite of mine.'

'Me tae!'

'I often saw them in Brighton.'

'Brighton!' She snuggled closer and with her free hand placed one of my hands on her breast. 'Did ye go by yersel?'

'Usually, yes.'

'How was that?'

'I preferred it.'

'That's a shame. Can ye no' manage they buttons?'

'What?'

'On ma blouse. There! It's quite easy.'

Again I cleared my throat.

'I never bother wi' a bra,' she told me.

Big Delia loomed above us, her bosom rolling over the top of the seat in front. 'Everybody pull up yer drawers, we're nearly there!' she shouted to the bus in general. 'And that means you tae, Ishbell!' Her plump hand, weighted with bracelets, pointed at the girl beside me as though cancelling a normal exemption. Then she raised anchors and went surging back down the bus, repeating the same message.

'Do you know that woman?' I asked, cautiously.

'A certainly do!'

'Your mother,' I guessed with fatal certainty.

'That's her,' said Ishbell.

Despite her mother's warning, the girl went right on doing what she was doing in the bus. And before we got *off* the bus – in exchange really for allowing me off – we

107

arranged a date for the pictures the following Wednesday.

She insisted that I was to have my tea at her house and gave me the name and address. Looking back on it, I can see – anyone can see – the inexorable pattern in all of this, but at the time I did not catch even a glint of the trap until the jaws started closing upon me at that address. It was a ground-floor flat and the door was open. In fact, there was no way of closing the door. And no point, since children were running in and out all the time. Big Delia Liddle was devoted to children. She gave *me* a big welcome, too, when eventually I found her stirring an enormous pot in the kitchen.

'Hello, son! Are ye comin' tae gie me a haun?'

'I did knock . . . at the front door.'

She laughed, 'Buggerall use that'll dae ye! The only man that chaps *ma* door is the rent man, so naebody'll answer it.' She left the pot and busied herself for a moment chopping vegetables with amazing speed and precision.

'Is Ishbell in?' I asked.

'Oh, it's Ishbell ye've tae see? A thought ye were Tony's pal.'

'Didn't she tell you I was coming?'

'Naw. But it disnae make any difference. A always make extra.'

'It smells delicious.'

She chuckled. ' "Delicious" – God, where did she get you?'

'On the bus.'

'She's an awful lassie, Ishbell!'

'You're very busy, Mrs Liddle. I'm sorry to disturb you.'

'Ye're no, botherin' me, son. Could dae this wi' ma eyes shut by touch and smell. Aye! An' wi' two dozen mad Italian waiters jumpin' across me shitin' theirsels.'

'You're a professional cook?'

'A was. Wan o' the best in ma day.'

'Why did you stop?'

'Tae look after ma weans, before the eldest were auld enough.'

'That's a pity.'

'Whit's a pity?'

'That you had to give up your career.'

'Career, b'God,' she snorted. 'You in trainin' tae be a manager?'

'No, an engineer.'

'A'd a thought ye could dae better for yersel'.'

'That's what I want to be. A marine engineer; so my father thought I should start on the Clyde.'

'Fancy!'

'This is where he served his time.'

'They've got nae shipyards in England, A suppose!'

'Yes. But a Clyde apprenticeship counts for more.'

'Then it's a wonder they hivnae diverted the bliddy river through London.'

I laughed. 'It wouldn't be the same.'

'Naw! It wid be cleaner. They'd see tae that.'

'And London already has a river.'

'Only the wan?' She raised her head briefly from the utensils and steam to remark, 'That's Tony, noo. A know their feet, every wan o' them.'

'I think I'll go and have a chat with him,' I said.

'Sure thing! You go an' hiv a chat.'

The younger children didn't seem at all curious about me as I wandered through the flat. They dodged past me or, height permitting, between my legs. In contrast to the spotless and orderly kitchen, the other rooms were a mess. As I picked my way between the debris of discarded toys and stacks of cardboard cartons a man's voice called, 'Is that you, Delia?' I called back, 'No!' and continued my search for Tony. He was wriggling out of very oily dungarees when I came upon him at the end of the lobby. He disposed of the overalls by kicking them under one of the two beds in the tiny room.

'Ye're here early.'

'I wasn't sure how long it would take me to find the place.'

He pushed past me. 'A've got tae get washed,' he said and went off towards the bathroom. 'C'mon!'

'That you, Delia?' called the voice again, but Tony ignored it. The voice was old, weary, and curiously tentative – as though the caller did not know if it was even possible to receive an answer.

'Is your father ill?' I asked Tony as he turned on the tap.

'How the hell dae A know? Whi' put that in yer mind?'

'The man, there, who was calling. Isn't he . . . ?'

'A've nae idea *who* he is.'

'Oh! Well, he seems to want something.'

'Aye. An' he'll get it, I expect.' He turned his dripping head towards me as he reached for a towel. 'Ma faither's at sea.'

'Is he an engineer?'

'That, A couldnae say.'

Elsewhere in the house children shouted and banged things, someone laughed and a radio played Fats Domino singing 'Blueberry Hill'. No two of the many people in that flat seemed to be together. They didn't know who was in and who was out or who was expected. I stared at Tony's narrow, thin shoulders as he faced the mirror, combing his hair – trying to coax it into a D.A. without much success because his pale hair was too wet. Never had I been so alien. And suddenly I felt sad for him, so vulnerably preoccupied with his hair, that he should be tied to this casual and – it seemed – dangerously unstable household. I was beginning to understand his habitual expression of worry.

'Whi's up wi' *your* face?' He was staring at my reflection in the mirror.

'I was . . . listening to the music.'

'Liar!' He prepared to brush his teeth.

'Why don't you brush your teeth *after* you've eaten?'

'A dae it then as well.'

'Oh.'

'Whi' *were* ye thinkin'?'

'I was wondering how many people there are in the house.'

'Includin' the weans?'

'Especially.'

'Well . . . when we're a' thegither – an' that's no' often – there must be . . . nine. Ten, maybe.'

'Are you the eldest?'

'Naw! A've got a big brother.' He chuckled. 'A *really* big brother. Neil. He's aboot twenty-five. Then there's me, an' then Ishbell.'

'What does Neil work at?'

'That's his business. If ye've got tae know, ask 'im.'

'I'm sorry. I didn't think it was . . . '

'The sooner ye get oot o' thinkin' that we're like you, the better.'

'Yes, I see that.'

'A don't mean tae chib ye, Billy. The thing is, you think ye kin talk aboot anything you know or want tae know. But there's a lot o' things aboot us, even *we* don't want tae know. Okay?' I nodded, but I didn't understand. Yet, I could believe it. Certainly there was something gravely secret about Tony.

'I don't mean to pry,' I said.

'Ye dae mean it,' he asserted. 'How other people live means a lot tae you, an' I'll tell ye how.'

'How? I mean, why?'

'Because you don't.'

'Don't what?'

'Live.' He grinned. 'How'd ye get on wi' Ishbell?'

'Fine. We're going to the cin . . . pictures.'

He held the toothbrush in mid-air and turned directly to me. 'When?'

'Tonight.'

'Don't think so,' he said. Again his voice was tight and bleak. 'She must've forgot.'

'What?'

'This is the night we start collectin' fur the Store Quarter.'

'Does she collect for that?'

'We a' collect fur that,' Tony said grimly and applied himself to his teeth with angry vigour. 'Bloody Store Quarter!' he spat.

Until then my knowledge of Quarter Days was limited to pleasing names such as Lady Day, Midsummer, Michaelmas and Christmas – which were of interest only to people living by the Inner Temple. For people living in Scotland, however, and on tick, they were days of judgment and

111

despair. These awful days were visited upon Co-op customers the first week in March, June, September and December.

Now I learned that there is no institution less co-operative than the Co-op when bills have to be paid. It was fear of Co-op retribution that led many people to deal instead with a middle-man – or middle-woman, such as Big Delia. That evening, as we ate her marvellous dinner, she marshalled her forces to *collect*. Beside her plate she had a huge pile of invoices and a tattered notebook.

'Neil! This time A want ye tae put the fear o' God in that wee sickener, Bilsland. Ye let him aff too light at Christmas.'

'His wife'd jist had a wean,' said Neil.

'Well, A'm no' gonnae wait tae the bliddy wean's auld enough tae work for ma money. You see 'im the night and tell 'im, Friday definite.' She handed over a pile of papers. 'There's a' his orders.'

Neil folded them and slid them under his place-mat at top position. He was, as Tony had told me, a *very* big brother with a slow, deep voice and the height and build to put the fear of God in anyone. 'Are they added up right?' he wanted to know. 'Sometimes they chisel me aboot the sums no' bein' added up right.'

Delia nodded. 'Tell him, if ye add it up again it might come tae mair.'

'An' tell him ye're comin' on *Saturday*, so that he'll be in on Friday,' said Tony.

'Right enough!' Ishbell agreed.

'Ishbell!' her mother said, 'if you dae Chisholm, Turner an' Gillies, ye'd still be in time fur the pictures.'

'She always gets the easy wans,' Tony complained.

'Turner's no' easy,' said Neil. 'She came at me wi' a knife, wance.'

'Tae stab ye in the *knee*?' Ishbell asked. Everyone laughed, including the old, white haired, haggard man to whom I was not introduced but was probably the unseen caller from the bedroom. Four of the younger children were also at the table; blessedly silent and well-behaved.

But Big Delia knew what she was doing. 'It's better tae send Ishbell tae the single women.'

'Aye, we don't want any payin' in kind,' said Tony under his breath, winking at me.

'Whi' was that?'

'A'm sayin' there'd be nae dividend in how they might pay Neil.'

'Watch yer mooth,' his mother warned.

'Whit's he talkin' aboot?' Neil asked. Evidently he was not the brightest of the family.

'Never mind. Tony's too smert fur his ain good.'

'An' naebody wid want tae pay him *except* wi' money,' said Ishbell, and for the briefest moment an expression of real pain creased her brother's face. If the girl noticed it she did not care.

'Do they always have the money?' I asked.

'No' always, but usually,' Tony said. 'If ye keep at them they remember where they put it, or where they can get it – if it comes tae the worst.'

'But what if they just haven't got it?'

'Then ma Maw has tae put it up hersel',' Ishbell told me.

Delia consulted her notebook. 'A'll dae Timmins, the two Kerrs, Devine an' Grant.'

Tony groaned. 'Aw, Ma! That leaves me wi' the same lot as last time.'

'Eat yer food!' Delia told him.

'But that's twice as many as Neil an' Ishbell!'

'Tony, son, A *know*! An' why? Because you're good at it.' She turned to me, with evident pride. 'If A ever started a protection racket that boy wid be worth a fortune.'

Ishbell said, 'They pay him because he's wee and skinny.'

'Naw!' his mother noted perceptively. 'They pay him because he's dangerous.'

'That's true,' Neil sighed regretfully.

'May I have some more vegetable, Mrs Liddle?'

'Certainly, son! Here ye are. Does your mother hiv any o' this bother wi' the Store Quarter?'

I choked at the thought of it. 'Hmmm . . . No.'

'Surely they've got the Co-op in England b'noo?'

'Oh, yes. They have it. But my mother doesn't shop there.'

'Silly wumman. It's a lot cheaper fur the groceries, at least.'

'As far as I know, she doesn't . . . shop for groceries. At all.'

The cutlery fell silent and each of those holding it stared at me for a long moment before Delia loudly filled the silence. 'An' how the hell dae yis eat?'

'We have a cook,' I said; aware – too late – that I was ruining the rest of the meal for all of us. I lowered my head to avoid their eyes, but not before I saw Tony and Ishbell exchange an identical slight nod and even slighter smile.

The great attraction of Ishbell, for me, was that she made all the effort. With her, the promise of sex was more of an affidavit. For someone as shy as I was then, such rare bounty could not be ignored. I went with her to see Chisholm, Turner and Gillies. As we walked along we took occasional advantage of the wretched street lighting in that part of the town. I also tried to find out more about such a remarkable family.

'It must be difficult for your mother coping with all this on her own,' I said.

'She's never on her own.'

'I mean, with your father at sea.'

'Ma father's in jail,' said Ishbell.

'But Tony told me he was at sea.'

'That's right. His father *is* at sea.'

'Then your mother was divorced?'

'Divorced?' Ishbell's soft, rather timid, voice betrayed a slight impatience. 'She never even got *married* for most o' us. Just Neil's father. She was married tae him; she says. But he died.'

We walked in silence for a while then I asked, 'What is your father in jail for?'

'Gettin' caught,' Ishbell said, weary of an old joke she had often told.

'Your mother must make things very awkward for all of you.'

'Awkward?'

114

'The way she lives.'

'My mother lives the way God made her,' Ishbell stated with no trace of timidity. 'And she's the kindest woman you're ever likely tae meet.'

'Yes, I'm sure she . . .'

'That's how all this started, y'know, wi' the Co-op. People came tae her and she got them what they needed. Kindness! And she was the one had tae pay up when they couldnae pay her. An' some o' them denied they got anything at a'! That's what ye get for kindness.'

'She's certainly a marvellous cook.'

'You'll know aboot that.'

'I'm sorry, I didn't mean to criticise her in the least.'

'It wisnae till Tony and me got older she could be sure o' gettin' her money. Somehow!'

'I just thought people must be critical of you, because of her.'

'If they are, they don't tell me.'

'Stop here a minute.'

'Let go! We havnae got time.'

'We've had time until now!'

'Ye've put me aff it.'

'What did I do?'

'Ye asked questions. Ye'd dae better if ye kept your mouth shut and your flies open.'

Tony didn't go up to Glasgow Tech. that Friday. It was final collection night. I didn't envy him the job of trudging around from door to door through the sleet and against a wild blustery wind. Even the short walk from Central to George Square left me miserable and exhausted. And, for once, I welcomed the stupefying heat in the basement of the Tech. We stood at the physics benches oozing pools of water on the polished wooden floor round our feet while steaming gently from the tops of our heads. The experiments had to be done by students in pairs, since it was the naive belief of our tutors that each would check and verify the written results obtained by the other. In practice we did the experiments then, quite separately, wrote the results which had been obtained five or ten years earlier by long-gone apprentices who'd prudently sold their notes. We did alter the odd fourth decimal point to avoid suspicion. My partner was Deanie.

'Got yer car yet?'

'No. I'm getting it next week.'

'We could'a done wi' it the night.'

'Yes. I could. Shall I do the experiment first?'

'Tell me this, how can they call it an experiment when people hiv been daein' it fur years?'

As I set up the apparatus the logic of the question bothered me. Deanie, however obscurely, had a point. 'I suppose it *is* an experiment for each person who does it for the first time.'

'Aye, except that – even the first time – we're expected to get that bloody stuff tae dae what somebody else *knows* it does.'

'Yes.'

'An' if we get it tae dae somethin' diff'rent – like a real experiment – we lose marks. Right?'

'Right.'

Pleased with my support he grew enthusiastic. 'Christ! Jist wance, I'd like tae make the bloody li'mus-paper turn *black*! They'd aw hiv kittens!' He laughed and stamped about in his puddle, delighted at the idea. 'Eh, Billy? We could put the entire li-mus-paper *industry* oot the gemm.'

'And the chemical industry,' I suggested, beginning to like Deanie.

'Sure!'

'What else?'

'A know how tae find gold.' He paused to see if I was interested.

'Tell me.'

'The elements hiv a' got their ain frequency y'see, so ye jist get a wee radio transmitter tuned tae exactly that frequency and point it at the hills. It beats paddlin' in burns wi' them big bowls.'

'Sounds a good idea.'

'There's jist wan thing – ye don't happen tae know the frequency o' gold, dae ye?'

'Seldom,' I told him. 'Anything else?'

'Listen! Last week A wis tellin' wee Liddle a great idea. See a' them things that make the wavy lines . . .'

'Oscilloscopes.'

He nodded eagerly. 'Whit's tae stop us convertin' them intae dinky wee television-sets?'

'We haven't got the time,' I told him. 'What did Tony Liddle say?'

'He said we'd make mair money jist floggin' the . . .'

'Oscilloscopes.'

'Aye. An' he should know – he's probably done it. A usually work wi' him, y'see. He's always thinkin' aboot makin' money, or stealin' it. Widnae surprise me if another sub post-office gets busted in Greenock th'night.'

I was incredulous. 'Rob a post-office?'

'He's done it before. Wisnae caught, but he done it all right.'

'At the beginning of March?'

'Don't think he's fussy. Naw, the Christmas before last, it wis. Tae get presents, maybe.'

'Do you know his family?'

'Know Big Delia. She's a case! She'll pick any auld ratbags aff the street and gie them a square meal if they look like they need it.'

'She seems a very . . . cheerful woman.'

'Oh, aye! When she's sober.'

Shortly, I was to discover what she was like when drunk. The train pulled into Greenock station and almost immediately, through the billowing steam at the barrier, I saw Tony waiting for me. He stood, hunched and intent, wearing a tightly belted raincoat. He watched me approach and even at that distance I could sense disaster.

'What's wrong?'

'I need your help, Billy.'

'What's happened?'

'A've no' been hame yet. Wid you come wi' me?'

'Now?'

'Aye.'

'It's nearly eleven o'clock. You could come to my digs; it's nearer.'

'That's no' the point.'

'We could talk there.'

'A don't jist want tae talk. Honest! Ye've got tae come wi' me.'

'Could I go to my digs first?'

'Naw. Right away. I've been waitin' on ye fur an hour an' a half!'

We moved out of the station and braced ourselves for a long walk against the wind and sleet. Tony said, 'If A go hame masel' she'll kill me.'

'Your mother?'

'A couldnae get it a'. The money. No even maist o' it!' His voice, pitched against the wind and traffic noise, had the edge of panic. 'She'll go bloody daft!'

'What can I do?'

'It'll help me. Wi' a stranger there she'll no . . . She'll no' dae anythin' . . . *desperate*.' Then he used a word I was perfectly sure he'd never used before in his life. 'Please!'

I went with him.

Delia could be heard as far away as the end of the street. The front door was wide open, letting the sound of her shrieks ricochet and amplify in the tunnel of the close before spreading wide in the open air. When Tony and I went in she was leaning over Ishbell who sat tight-lipped at the table, still wearing her raincoat and hood. Delia herself seemed to have risen from bed. She wore a thin, low-cut petticoat which exposed the threatening mass of her breasts and, over it, a long untied dressing-gown. Her feet were bare and when she looked up to confront us we could see the tears of sheer anger running down her cheeks. She stumbled a little towards Tony. 'Oh, ye've come back ya sleekit' wee bastard! Well?'

'Ma! Couldnae get it a' . . . .'

'*You* couldnae!'

'They hivnae got it, honest.'

'How much!' She rushed at him and gripped his hair. 'Holy God, ya runt, how much?'

Tony stumbled against me and I, moving further into the room, caught sight of the drained faces of two younger

118

children hiding behind the armchair at the fire. Tony cried, 'Oh, ma hair! Don't! Maw, don't!'

'How much?'

'A only got . . .'

'*Only*!'

' . . . Simpson an' . . . Ooooh! White.'

Delia roared, 'White! Shite! Ye got nothin'. An' that wee hooer didnae get wan o' *hers*! Did ye?' She whirled around and slapped Ishbell squarely across the face.

'Mammy!' the girl cried. Her chair toppled over.

'Stop!' I shouted but my voice was constricted with fear.

Delia ignored me and almost trotted up and down the room in frustrated fury.

'Whi' am A tae dae! Tell me! Whi' am A tae dae? An' whi'll happen tae the weans? C'm'ere, hen. C'm'ere tae yer mother.' She halted unsteadily and spread her arms wide for one of the small children. The child didn't budge.

'She's frightened, Maw,' Tony protested.

Delia bawled with all her might, 'COME HERE!'

Before worse could happen Ishbell scrambled up and delivered the hostage to her mother's arms. 'There. There ye are, Mammy. She wis jist frightened.'

Delia clasped the child to her and stood swaying in the middle of the room. 'Efter a' A've done for them, this is whi' A get! Ma weans'll be taken on the Parish. Poor wean, d'ye understand? Ye're Mammy's finished.' Her voice swooped to the maudlin as she stroked the child, but almost immediately leapt again to rasp, 'An whose fault is it? Whose bastard'n fault?' She lunged again at Tony but tripped slightly on the trailing cords of her dressing gown. I grabbed the child and set her down out of reach. Delia kicked her foot free of the cord then kicked at Tony. 'Yours! Comin' back here wi' nothin'! Nothin'! Nothin'. Oh, you'll rue this day. A'll make ye rue the day ye welched on ye're mother!'

'A cannae help it, Maw.' Tony tried to sound soothing but the unaccustomed attempt was not convincing.

'Ye'll hiv tae help it! There's nothin' fur ye but that. An' before Monday. D'ye hear me? Before Monday or your life'll no be worth livin'.' She gripped his hair with both hands, forcing his head back, and screamed in his face, 'D'ye hear me?'

Tony did not struggle and he let his arms hang, swinging, at his sides.

'Mrs Liddle, maybe if . . . '

'Shut your face! Whi' are ye daein' here anyway? Lookin' fur *anither* cook, eh? Ya stuck-up English pig! Got a place fur me in yer scullery? Christ, that's a' A'll be fit fur efter this, if A'm no' emptyin' piss-pots in jail.'

Ishbell tried to placate her. 'Neil got a' his.'

'He did! He did that!' Her tone altered and for a moment it seemed she would be diverted. 'He's a good boy. An' good tae me!' But then she resumed with evil intensity, 'An' he's a *decent* boy, because he wis put intae me in *ma man's bed* – no' up against a wa' like you. An' you! Ya clap-scarred, poxy bastards!' She staggered past us, pushing Tony aside, and shouted down the lobby, 'Neil! Neil!' She stood swaying and hanging onto the edge of the door until he appeared. He must have been lying in bed listening to all of this for he wore only a pair of underpants. Delia threw herself in his arms, weeping.

'It'll be a'right, Ma,' Neil said. 'We'll get the money somehow.' Awkwardly, he stroked her head and she erupted in a sustained sobbing wail.

Neil repeated, 'A'right.' He tried to lead her to a chair while she flexed her hands gripping his shoulders and rubbed her face against his chest. Very softly, almost crooning, he reassured her, 'We'll get it. We'll get it.'

Tony whispered urgently, 'Ishbell! You'd better get tae yer bed.'

'Whi' aboot him!'

'Billy's a'right wi' me. Go on! When she's quiet. An' take they weans.'

Hidden by Neil, and with his complicity, Ishbell took the two young children out of the room. Unfortunately, she tried to close the door behind her and the sound alerted Delia.

'Whi's that?'

'Nothing, Ma,' Neil tried to block her view. 'Sit there.'

But she surged out of the chair. 'Where . . . Where is

she? Skinned oot?' Tony stood with his back pressed against the door. She would have thrown him aside but Neil caught her arms and held her back. Thwarted, she wrenched her head from side to side, roaring, 'I'll get ye! A'll *swing* fur ye, ya rotten wee spunk-bag!' Now all her venom was directed at Tony.

'But A've got you, toerag . . .'

'Maw! Don't!' he pleaded.

'Don't whi'?' She threw off Neil's grip. 'Let go! Neil, son, get me a knife.'

'That's enough,' Neil protested, moving in front of her.

'Get me a knife! A'm gonnae mark that skinny weasel for good!'

'Naw, he'll get the money. He will.' Again the big man tried to soothe her.

'Where?' she cried. 'Where?'

'He'll get it.'

'If he disnae A'll end 'im, sure as Christ!'

Neil continued to stroke her. 'Take it easy. We'll manage. There!'

I looked at Tony who had moved to the far side of the room. He nodded at the door and I opened it and, as his elder brother slowly moved Delia back to the chair, he slipped out. She knew he had escaped but now, it seemed, she was even more aware of the warmth and strength of the arms that held her. She began to enjoy being comforted as though not by her son but by this desirable man who embraced her. She pressed herself against him and he seemed prepared to take on a new role.

'Aw,' she sighed. 'You're a fine big fella!'

'Aye. Come on, sit doon.'

'Ower here. Oooh, A love ye!'

'A know.'

It started like a predetermined ritual. All this had happened before and would happen again. Neil knew how to calm his mother. Horrified, I moved carefully out of the room.

Tony was sitting on the edge of the bath and he beckoned me in. 'Lock the door.' I turned and pushed the substantial bolt. 'That's the only door that locks in this hoose,' he said.

121

Then, feeling more secure, he slumped forward resting his elbows on his knees. 'Oh, God! Whi' am A gonnae dae?'

'She seems quieter now.'

'For how long? There's the rest o' th' night and the morra.'

'How much money should have been collected?'

'A'thegither?'

'Yes?'

'Too much! Faur too much. A've got a list.'

As he stretched to delve into his coat pocket I noticed that the toe-cap of one of his shoes was practically ripped off and his feet were soaked through.

'Roughly, how much?'

'Hivnae added them up yet. But there ye are. There's the exact amount, against each name. Tried everythin'! They hivnae got it tae gie me!'

I looked at the names. 'There must be over a dozen people. That's . . . thirty two pounds, seventeen, forty, twenty one . . .'

'Don't tell me!' he protested. 'Add it up.'

'It comes to nearly four hundred pounds!'

'Ohhhh!' He slumped forward again. 'She'll kill me. She'll kill me. A darenae face her again.'

'I'd no idea it could be as much as that.'

'Aye. It's the March quarter, y'see. Noo's when they should pay for a' the stuff they got at Christmas. The March quarter's always the worst.'

'Four hundred pounds.'

'If A could even get a *loan*. But nae bugger's gonnae lend tae me, or the *likes* o' me!' He reached out and gripped my hand. 'Oh, Billy! Whi' am A gonnae dae?'

'I'll give you the money,' I said.

He didn't seem to take it in. '*Lend* it tae me?'

'No. I'll give it to you. Then you won't have to do anything . . . stupid, to try and pay it back.'

He stood up, staring at me with a dazed, almost wild, expression. 'You'll *gie* it tae me! The whole four hundred? But where'll *you* get it?'

'I've been saving up to buy a car,' I told him. 'I was going to buy it outright for six hundred pounds.'

His response came most acutely. 'Then ye'll still hiv enough tae lay doon a deposit.'

'I could, but I won't.'

'An' ye're gonnae gie me maist o' the money ye saved! Billy, ye've nae idea whi' that means tae me.'

'Do you want to go and tell your mother now?'

'Naw! She'd never believe us. She'll no' believe us till A've got the cash in ma haun.'

'I'll get it for you when the banks open on Monday morning.'

'That's great! So, A'll be doon at the yerd gate at dinner-time.'

'All right.' I unbolted the door.

'Billy!'

'Yes?'

'A want ye tae understand . . . wi' ma mother . . . she's that *proud* y'see. And the drink. She's no' hersel when she's'd too much tae drink. Thing is, she'll no' be right sober tae the quarter's by. Her nerves are no' up tae it, noo.'

'What about your nerves?'

'Aye, but A hivnae had her life.'

'I can't understand why you stay here.'

'Whi's that?' For the first time that evening the bleak, hostile, tone was back in his voice.

'I don't know how you can bear it, here!'

'Where else wid A be?'

'You could get digs. I'm in digs.'

'So ye are. But *your* mother's no' at her wits' end thinkin' o' weys tae keep a' they weans, an' us, under wan roof.'

'No.'

'No! *Your* mother disnae rely on the Store dividend tae feed them. An' she doesnae depend on *you* for any damn thing at a'.'

'Not at the moment. But she expects a great deal from me in the future.'

He expelled his breath disdainfully. 'How dae ye get tae the future? Tell me that, Billy. How dae I *get* tae the future when A don't even know there's gonnae *be* a future?'

'I mean, when you're qualified.'

'Oh, A'm gettin' qualified all right.'

'Not like this.'

'If ye're me, ye cannae pick an' choose.'

'Other families get along.'

'Sure. But A wis born intae *this* family. An' there's naebody thought o' changin' it – jist tae suit me.'

'You are all separate people, though.'

'No. This family depends on each other for everythin'. Nae other wey!'

'Yes. I understand.'

'A'm *responsible* here!' Suddenly the strain caught up with him and he was weeping. 'A'll . . . always be . . . re . . . responsible.' He turned away and stared at his own swimming eyes in the mirror.

That Friday night taught me a number of things, but I did not learn them. Since I'd been educated at a public school, the idea of being a separate person from my family was forced upon me at an early age. My father was often abroad and my mother devoted most of her time to music. Clearly, they were quite separate people, too. The idea of a family as a self-destroying, self-renewing organic unit was quite alien to me when I saw it in action that Friday. On the Saturday morning I went to the car showroom and told the salesman I'd changed my mind. He didn't take it at all well. In fact, he seemed more disappointed than I was. He stared through the plate-glass after me, like a man betrayed. By staying away from my digs for the rest of the day I hoped to avoid whatever news of disaster there might be from the Liddles.

Sunday I spent studying but couldn't concentrate for straining to hear that knock on the door heralding Tony or Ishbell or even worse – I saw it clearly – the white face of one of those terrified children. I asked my landlady, Mrs Mulvenny, if she was a 'Store' customer. She said she was, but if I wanted her to get me something I'd have to wait until Tuesday because Monday was the Store Quarter. I told her I knew that. On Monday morning I applied to the foreman for a 'Pass Out' on 'vital family business' and withdrew my savings. I felt like a thief, carrying all my own money back through the streets. At lunch-time, Tony was waiting for me at the yard gate and I handed over my only chance of insulating myself from my apprenticeship.

It was on the following Sunday that I had a visitor. 'Mrs Liddle!'

'Hello, son. How are ye gettin' on?'

'I'm fine. How are you? Please, sit down.' She really looked quite striking in a dark blue wool suit, a hat with a veil and – to my astonishment – gloves. 'You're looking very well.'

'Thanks. Where will A put this?'

'What is it?'

'It's a special cake I've made for ye.'

'Thank you very much. I'll . . . put it here.'

'A've come because A thought A should apologise fur bein' in a bit o' a temper when ye came tae see Tony last week.'

'Oh!'

'A wis that worried, y'know, aboot collectin' fae the customers.'

'Yes.'

'An' then wi' Tony kiddin' me on aboot no' gettin' the money – that wis a silly thing tae dae.'

'That I did?'

'Naw, naw. You didnae dae anything. A'm sayin', *Tony*. You were there when he said it. That he couldnae get the money.'

'Yes, I heard him say that.'

'Well – he had it a' the time! Collected fae every wan. He wis at the Store first thing on Monday, waitin' fur me, an' we cleared the whole account.'

'That must have been a great relief to you.'

'A'm tellin' you it wis! Anyway – A'm very sorry if A upset ye when ye were in at the hoose. An' A hope ye enjoy that wee present.'

'I'm sure I shall.'

'An' mind! The next time ye're passin' you come in an' see us. The weans were a' tickl't wi' the funny wey you talk.'

'Really! Er . . . I didn't see Tony at the college this week.'

'Naw, he didnae go. Hisnae been at work either. Seems tae hiv caught an awful bad chill, so A'm keepin' him in his bed. Better get back an' see if he needs anythin'.' She rose with ease onto her perilously high heels.

'Oh, please don't go yet. I think Mrs Mulvenny is making some tea for you.'

'I'll tell her no' tae bother.' She laughed – for a moment very much the grand lady visiting the needy. 'Tae be honest A hivnae got the time.' She moved to the door. 'But whenever you want a good meal, remember, ye're always welcome.'

I stood in the centre of the room, dazed. How could this possibly be the same woman? And, if it was, how could she possibly describe the raging behaviour I'd seen as 'a bit of a temper'? Yet it was she. And there was the cake to prove it. And the venomous foul-mouthed virago *was* the rather superior woman now chatting, somewhat condescendingly, to my landlady. Obviously Tony hadn't told her he'd got the money from me. Considering his status in the family and his sense of responsibility I could understand his need to claim a full score as chief collector. What was absolutely inconceivable was her belief that Tony was just kidding her when he reported that he'd failed. Who, I wondered, in his right mind, would kid Delia, about *money*, when she was drunk! I went into the lobby and called her back.

'Excuse me, Mrs Liddle!'

'Aye? What is it . . . er, Billy?' She re-entered the room.

'That *was* a silly trick for Tony to play on you – pretending most of his customers hadn't paid.'

'As long as it was a trick. A suppose he jist wanted tae know whi' A'd say.'

'Yes. And he certainly found out.'

Her tone hardened. 'Whi' was it ye wanted tae ask me, Billy?'

'Well, you see . . . I was sure he meant it. That he wasn't pretending.'

'That's because you don't know him as well as me.'

'I hardly know him at all.'

'Is that right? Oh, A thought you an' him were great pals.'

'I wondered if, perhaps, you'd seen any of his customers since then.'

'Make a point o' it, son! His customers are ma customers. Efter the Quarter A go roon and see them a'. Tae thank them, an' that. An' tae let them know, if there's anything mair they want me to get fur them they've only tae ask.'

'And those that Tony collects from had all paid?'

Delia grew impatient. 'Son, A don't think you're followin' this very well. That's three times A've telt ye. *Aye*! Tony got the money fae every wan o' them. D'ye understand noo?'

'Yes. Now I understand.'

She turned, once more, to go. 'Well, A'm glad A've cleared that up fur ye,' she said; then added not entirely under her breath, 'Bring a cake an' get the bliddy Means Test!'

'Good bye, Mrs Liddle, and thank you.'

'Right ye are.'

Tony got over his chill by the following Friday and he was back at the Tech. – again partnering Deanie. He gave me a wave across the bristling laboratory benches. I nodded, but waited until the others had left the compartment in the train back before letting him know what I knew. He was far from overcome with shame. He adjusted his position in the corner seat so that he faced me diagonally across the compartment.

'A wid've been a mug *no*' tae take that money aff you,' he said.

'But you didn't need it!'

'Wrong. A need it. Ma *mother* didnae need it – this time.'

'What do you need it for?'

'Debts. Gam'lin'. Fines. You've got nane a them tae take care o', hiv ye?'

'But all that's your own fault.'

'Sure. But A cannae pay them by sayin' sorry.'

'You could say sorry to me.'

'Wid that be enough?'

'No. But it's the least you could do.'

'Sorry, Billy, that a took ye're money. Ishbell's sorry tae.'

'Ishbell?'

He gave a little bark of a laugh. 'She's sorry because it wisnae her that got it.'

'Did she know what you were doing?'

'Christ, fella, we were *baith* ontae ye. Set ye up for it. You were gonnae lose that money wan way or the other. An' A must say if ye'd tried the other, ye'd a got mair satisfaction fur yer money than a cake.'

'I see.'

For a few moments there was only the sound of the train's progress as I stared out of the window and he watched me staring out of the window.

The silence seemed to annoy him. 'Ye were askin' fur it!' he protested. 'Talkin' aboot buyin' cars, saved up, cash down. Whi' the hell dae ye expect?'

'I gave you the money because I was sorry for you.'

'A *know*.'

'I would have done anything to prevent a night like that one happening again.'

He snorted. 'Again? When Big Delia's drunk, a night like that is rou*tine*. It's no' jist the Store Quarter that annoys her, y'know. The'night, maybe, when a go in – it'll be the same thing. Different reason, but the same wumman you saw that night.'

'You're going back to that?'

'Likely.'

'How can you bear it?'

'Practice. Never known anythin' else.'

'Then you deserve the money.'

He nodded and seemed affected by that thought. 'Aye,' he sighed. 'Better still – A deserve tae hiv been born *you*!'

Now that I knew the Liddle family, I seemed to see or hear of them all the time. The local paper frequently reported the various social enterprises of Mrs Liddle and often Big Delia's bright-eyed face leapt at me from press photographs of one line-up or another. Now and then I saw Ishbell in the street and one hot summer day when I was on my way to Glasgow she occupied the seat in front of me on the bus.

'How's the family?' I asked.

'No' quite ready yet,' she said, and invited me to lean over the back of the seat. She was pregnant.

'Oh! Congratulations!'

'Tae the faither?'

'No, to you.'

'Huh!' She shook her head and turned to face the front. 'It wisnae my idea. I'm just too good natured.'

I was rather shocked by the observation but Elsie, the girl who was with me, gaffawed with delight.

As Tony had predicted, I did pass all the necessary exams and so, with day-release, my weekly visits to the Tech. were over. Tony himself was once or twice reported in the paper. In the exam results I noted that he'd passed his L.N.C. In police court proceedings, I noted that he was less successful at burglary. We didn't meet again for a long time. But, though many Quarter Days went by, not one passed without acute unease on my part. So I had the Liddles in mind when Archie Hemple stopped at my board in the Drawing Office.

'Have ye heard aboot Big Delia?' he asked.

'She's started a protection racket,' I suggested.

'No. She's dead.'

'What!'

'Some weans ran intae the polis office this mornin'. They went tae the hoose an' found her stabbed. They've lifted Neil for questionin'.'

'It wasn't Neil,' I said.

'How dae you know.

'He didn't *care* enough.'

'Whi' are ye talkin' about? They think he might have *stabbed* her.'

'That's what I mean. He wouldn't.'

The police went through the usual elaborate shadow-boxing exercise in their information to the newspapers. And the newspapers, as usual, managed to make all those involved seem quite unreal. I knew Tony would give himself up and, before the end of the week, he did.

'It wis Tony, efter a',' Archie marvelled. 'Can ye credit it?'

'Easily.'

'Whi' wid make him dae a thing like that?'

'Self defence?'

'It's no' somethin' tae joke aboot. She wis an awful kind wumman, Big Delia.'

'Yes, and she expected as much as she gave.'

'Ah, well,' said Archie. 'Ye can never tell whit a homo's gonnae dae.'

'Pardon?'

'Tony Liddle.'

'Yes. What did you say about him?'

Archie was obviously astonished at my ignorance. 'Ye mean you didnae know?'

'What?'

'That he's a homo?'

'You don't mean homicidal?'

'Naw! A mean homosexual.'

'How do you know that?'

'Because a pal o' mine used tae get intae him, regular.'

Perhaps unjustly, I immediately thought of Deanie. 'I don't believe it,' I said.

'Ho!' Archie scoffed. 'There's many a wan – that should know – will tell ye the same thing. And some o' them got money out of him tae keep it quiet.' He nodded firmly. 'I'm tellin' ye – real Mamma's boy, wee Tony.'

Rather weakly I commented, 'I didn't know that you knew so many homosexuals.'

'Naw, *they're* no'. He is.'

'I see.'

Unwilling to contemplate the possibility that some of my money had gone to pay blackmail, I disregarded this information. But later in the year, when all the circumstances were set out at the trial, that fact could not be avoided. Nor could the facts of the murder. Tony's lawyers claimed mitigating circumstances. Neil, Ishbell and several neighbours testified to that and he got fifteen years.

Some months later I had an appointment in Glasgow to be fitted for my Merchant Navy uniform. I applied for a visitor's pass to Barlinnie the same day. Tony, in his uniform, looked even younger than before.

'Well, Billy! You're the first, apart fae the family.'

'How is the family?'

'All right, a suppose. Ishbell's runnin' the hoose and Neil's got a steady job.'

'Good.'

'So they don't really need me.'

'It's a big family to provide for.'

'Aye, but Ishbell's no' proud. She takes charity. That's somethin' ma Maw wid never dae.'

I was shocked that he should mention her, but foolishly determined to show that I was not shocked. 'No. Your mother was a very . . . enterprising woman.'

'There wis nae stoppin' her,' he said admiringly. I couldn't think how to respond to that and we faced each other in silence for a few moments. Then he asked, 'Did ye ever get a car?'

'No. And now I don't need one. I'm going to sea.'

'Ye didnae need wan then, either. Ye jist *wantit* wan.'

'That's true.'

'So?'

'What?'

'Whi' did ye dae wi' the money ye had left? A often wondered aboot that?' His cold eyes were friendly enough. He just wanted to know if I'd wasted money he could have had.

'I invested it.'

'Invested! Holy God, there's nae beatin' you either.'

'How are they treating you here?'

'No' bad.' He repeated it loudly for the officers. 'No' bad at a'.'

'And the family visits you.'

'*Only* the family. Why did you come tae see me?'

'Because I . . . well . . . curiosity, I suppose.'

'Aye. Ye were always a nosey bugger. So – whi' dae ye want tae know that ye don't know already?'

'Whatever you'd like to tell me.'

'Right. A'll tell ye this. She wis the only human bein' that gave a damn aboot me. An' the only wan ever *likely* tae. Wi' her gone A'm no' missin' much bein' in here.'

I believed him. At least, I believed that he thought so. There was nobody now to test his ability; and no one to whom he must prove it.

Perfect Pitch

Most people who've heard of *The Tales of Hoffmann* limit their familiarity to the Barcarolle. The record I never tire of playing is from another tale – that of Olympia, Hoffmann's first love. She is a fabulous doll who comes to life; and sings a most testing aria to prove it. My record of Olympia's aria is very worn because I often want to be reminded of Greenock. And she does it; bringing back the smell of tarred rope and the sound of a factory whistle – each of them potent Greenock locators on my map of the interior.

Other people are content enough to find Greenock where it is – strung out along a narrow shore on the rainier side of the Clyde estuary. There's a saying: 'If you can see Greenock, it's going to rain. If you can't, it is raining.' It was there I served my apprenticeship, twenty-five years ago. It was there I met Elsie.

Quite near the shipyard where I worked there was a rope factory which employed a large number of girls. They were a rough and ready lot, occasionally foul-mouthed but always merry – or 'cheery', as they say there. During the lunch-break they lined up on the wall outside the factory, reeking of tar, to survey whatever male 'talent' might be passing. They were not easily pleased. And not reticent in alluding to – or shouting to each other – the precise nature of their misgivings. When I was nineteen I was barely brave enough – even supported by Frank – to run that gauntlet. And it was only for his sake that we did it. He fancied one of those girls.

'Which one?' I asked him.

'Her in the middle, beside the gate.'

'With the red hair?'

'Naw! The quiet wan, beside her. Come on.'

Before dodging through the traffic in Frank's impetuous wake, I paused in the bustling midday street to fix the target. She had dark hair and was, I suppose, the most demure of the bunch; which is to say, the least raucous – which is not to say a great deal. I joined Frank on the other pavement and we sauntered past them with hands deeply delved in dungaree pockets. Our casual passing was logged, interpreted and loudly noted by the red-haired girl.

'Hey, Ada!' she shouted to Frank's fancy, who sat immediately beside her.

'Whit?'

''Er's them two again! D'ye think they're auld enough tae be ower it?'

'Ower whit?'

'The knot, ya stupit bitch!' She gave a yelping laugh then shouted directly at us, 'Hey, son, are ye?'

I guessed that she was enquiring about a facility we acquired at puberty.

'Whit dae ye want?' Frank shouted back.

The one who was not Ada gave an ecstatic shriek. 'Ooooh! Whit dae A want? As if you could gie me anything A'd want!'

Ada said, 'Leave him alane, Elsie!'

Elsie tossed her red hair – which was too short and frizzy to convey much hauteur. 'A've every intention o' leavin' him alane. Christ! That wee fella must be still wankin' dry.'

'You watch ye gub!' warned Frank.

'You watch it, you've got a better view.'

Frank put his shoulder behind mine and, with a brisk shove, urged me out of range. 'Come on.'

But Elsie hadn't dealt with me yet. She called after us. 'Does ye're big mate no' talk? Whit's he haud'n on tae?'

'Nothing,' I called back.

Elsie seized on that. 'Another wan wi' nothin' in his pocket! Honest tae God, Ada, we never hiv any luck. They must breed bloody eenochs in that yerd!'

Correcting the pronunciation I replied, 'Eunuchs!' but she chose to treat it as confirmation.

'There ye are.' She jabbed Ada with her elbow. 'Whit did A tell ye? He gives in!' Her loud laughter was interrupted by the high piercing note of the factory whistle. 'Holy God! Times up a'ready.' She jumped off the wall and, as she paced slowly backward through the factory gate, continued to call to me, 'See ye the morra, son. Maybe somethin'll sprout durin' the night . . . if ye watter it!'

That was our first encounter and, to be honest, I wasn't very hopeful about Frank's chances for a lasting relationship. But in that, as in so many other things, I had misjudged the spirit of the occasion. In my simple English way, I had mistaken the sound of insult for an intention of insult. Frank knew better.

'Well, whi' d'ye expect her tae say? "Pleased to meet you"?'

'Maybe not. But your dark-haired one didn't say anything.'

'Aye, she did.'

'What?'

'She tell't the red-heidit lassie tae leave me alane.'

Frank knew what that meant. He knew what everything meant. When I'd come up from England to start my apprenticeship it was Frank who took pity on my ignorance of the language. He thought my accent was mildly hilarious and wondered how long I could keep it up. And he was very sympathetic when he found out I couldn't help it. Anyway – he knew that if the dark-haired girl told the red-haired girl to leave him alone, it meant that – however distantly – *she* fancied *him*. Next morning while working together at the marking-off table, we discussed strategy.

'It wid be easier if they werenae always thegither.'

'Yes. And maybe it would be better if you walked by on your own.'

'Naw, naw.' Frank saw the danger in that. 'Then she wid think that I fancy *her*.'

'I thought you did!'

Frank was immediately belligerent. 'Whit if A dae?'

'Well . . . ' The intricacies of this were beginning to tire me. 'Wouldn't that help?'

He promptly took refuge in our common task. 'Are you supposed tae be workin' on this or no'? Whit aboot that corner ye havenae pasted?'

For a few silent minutes I set about my job of applying the whitewash to the surface of the brass plate; on which Frank, when it had dried, could mark off the drilling pattern with a metal 'scribe', hammer and dab. It was a very soothing occupation and soon I felt the conversation could be continued.

'Do you want me to go with you, then?'

It was too soon. Frank was still on the defensive. 'Look Bill, if you've got somethin' else t'dae, don't bother yer arse.'

'No. Nothing.'

'A widnae want ye tae be affrontit,' he said, using the hammer and dab as punctuation, 'wi' aw they bad lassies usin' sweery words.'

'I don't mind that. I think it's quite funny.'

'They're no' daein it tae be funny.'

'So – we'll go by again today at lunchtime?'

'Dinner-time!' Frank corrected wearily.

'Yes.'

'An' you can chaff the ither yin.'

'What?'

'The red-heidit wan – she's yours!' he expansively granted.

This was rather more than I was willing to do on his behalf. 'What shall I say to her?'

'Tell her whit ye've got in yer pocket.'

'I think she knows.'

Frank gave a shout of laughter. 'By God, she knows! I'll bet she's seen mair o' them than a lavatry wall.'

'She seems very defensive.'

'What?'

'As if she were afraid of something.'

'Get away!'

'Afraid of being taken seriously.'

He did not spare that idea a moment's thought. He said,

'She'd be a nice enough lassie, if her mouth was shut. Tell her that. Maybe she'll try it.' Spread flat on his stomach across the condenser plate he applied a series of delicate taps to the pointillist drilling design. 'Anyway, you've tae keep her muzzled while I talk tae the ither yin.'

'Ada.'

'How d'ye know that?'

'That's what Elsie called her.'

'Who the hell's Elsie?'

'Mine. Weren't you listening?'

He reared up by arching his back. 'Ada? Funny name, that!'

'Maybe you'll get used to it, when you know her better.'

He gave me a very lewd grin. 'There's only wan thing A want tae get used tae, when A know her better,' he growled, and executed a few humping movements on the whitewashed surface.

I sighed at this display. 'Frank! It's me.'

'An' whitsa different about you?'

'You don't have to *bluff* me.'

He threw down the hammer with an angry clang. 'And you don't hiv tae *tell* me. Right.'

'Sorry.'

Frank had integrity, there's no denying that. If you called his bluff, he'd admit it. As long as you didn't try it very often.

He was short, energetic and wiry; with wiry hair and a big nose which he'd aim at you in a menacing way – as though he'd already released the safety catch. Come to think of it, there was a hair-trigger immediacy about everything he did. For him, Do It Now was the only way to live. So, phase two of operation Ada could not be delayed. I paused on the waste ground outside the canteen to arm myself. Frank was already well ahead, walking towards the rope factory. As I caught up with him he instructed me. 'Try and get them tae separate – okay?'

'You mean, pull mine off the wall?'

'As long as ye get her aff ma back.'

Elsie saw us coming from a long way off, but waited until we were comfortably within earshot before loudly asking her companion, 'Hey, Ada! Hiv you got yer horns oot, hen?'

'Naw, how?'

''Cause here's a coupla peasants starin' at us.'

Frank's urgent shoulder indicated that I get on with the chaff. 'Hello', I smiled. 'Your name's Elsie, isn't it?'

'Holy God!' the girl exclaimed. 'It's no' a peasant at a'. It's an English nancy-boy.'

'No – I'm not.'

'Well, ye *sound* English.'

'I've got something for you,' I declared.

'In there? A doubt it.'

From my dungaree pocket I drew the long stem of the foxgloves which abounded behind the canteen, 'There you are!'

'Jesus!' She stared at the flower and then at me as though I were mad. Clearly, I had gained some sort of advantage. 'Whit am A supposed tae dae wi' this?' she asked.

'Clench it between your teeth.'

She laughed with genuine amusement and, I thought, appreciation at the suggestion. And she continued to hold the flower in her hand while she answered my few pointless questions about her work. Meanwhile, Frank did his best with Ada at close range. Before long, my conversation with Elsie began to pall on both of us. I glanced at my watch once or twice and she threw back her head to catch some rare sunlight under her chin. Then, not a moment too soon, it seemed we heard the Works whistle. All the girls, except Elsie, scattered and ran for the Works gate, to be in while the whistle was still blowing and avoid being 'quartered'. That is, losing quarter of an hour's wages. The whistle faded and Elsie brought her head forward to face me; her eyes sparkling, a mischievous grin on her face. 'Ye're damn all good at the patter, Billy, I'll tell you that,' she told me. 'Get yer mate tae gie ye a few tips.' She jumped down from the wall and sauntered alone through the gate. She was safely inside, unquartered, when the real whistle sounded.

'What the hell are they playin' at?' Frank wanted to know.

'It's exactly on time.'

'But that's the second time they've blew it.'

I shook my head delightedly. 'No. The first time it was Elsie. She hit exactly the right note, on the button, and held it!'

I wish I could say that *gradually* it occurred to me where this remarkable ability of Elsie's might lead. The slow realisation of her potential value would be much more interesting. But it didn't occur to me gradually at all. It struck me instantly. Falseness is very hard to spot, but who doesn't know the truth when they hear it?

The truth was that Elsie had an amazingly accurate, pure and powerful singing voice. More could be done with it than imitating factory whistles. Probably I would not have reached such an adamant conclusion, even at nineteen, if I had not been brought up in a 'musical' atmosphere. My mother devoted a lot of her time to music – mainly operatic – and it was she who had told me of that rarest of creatures; that fabulous unicorn among singers – the voice which has perfect pitch. That, as I say, was what I knew instantly. Proving it took much longer. To start with, it meant making a date with Elsie.

She agreed readily enough – at our third tryst by the Rope Works wall – but she wanted to see *The Inn Of The Sixth Happiness* which had recently opened its doors in Greenock, and I wanted to spend the evening in a particular cafe.

'Whi' fur?'

'So that we can talk.'

'Talk!' Not her idea of a date, apparently. 'Whi' d'ye want tae talk aboot?'

'Different things.'

'How, different? That cafe hasnae even got a jukebox.'

'I know.'

'Be a real cheap night fur ye, that.' She again essayed the disdainful tossing of her head and again her short hair refused to swish. It only bounced a little round the ears. It occurred to me that she couldn't know how short her hair was.

'We could go on to the second house at the cinema.'

'And miss the *wee* picture?' she exclaimed – incredulous.'

'Well – it's Ingrid Bergman you want to see, isn't it?'

'Dae A hell! It's Curt Jürgens A want tae see.'

So, we settled for that; missing the supporting feature but seeing all of Curt Jürgens. The choice of that particular cafe was part of my underhand plot to seduce Elsie into believing in herself as a singer. It was a modest little shop owned by a man who played subdued and *tuneful* music on a gramophone under the counter. I took a record with me. As we walked in, Elsie made it plain that she was not impressed with the dim interior or the softness of the music. She halted just over the threshold. 'Christ Almighty! Has there been a death in the family?'

'I think it's quite pleasant.' I urged her forward to a table.

'Oh, aye. Pleasant enough – as long as we get oot before "Abide wi' Me".'

'Do you sing?'

'How? Are ye gonnae take a collection?'

'No. I mean . . . *can* you sing?'

'Don't be daft,' she said, spacing her forearms on the table as though at a card school. 'Everybody can sing.'

To her that was a fact and the subject needed no further comment. She looked around at the few other, older people in the cafe, then – making the best of a bad job – brightly back at me. 'Now! Wha' d'ye want tae talk about?'

'Well . . . you!'

'Wha' d'ye want tae know aboot me?' She twisted round in her chair with the intention of obtaining service. 'Where the hell's the man?'

'I think he's in the store-room.'

'He's quite right. It'll be livelier in there, A should think. Wha' *aboot* me?'

'What age are you?'

She laughed. 'Don't worry aboot it. I'll tell them A led ye on.'

'No, but really?'

'Sixteen, how?'

'You seem older.'

'I should bloody well hope so! Or A've wastit' money on this make-up. Who dae A remind you o'?'

'Amelita Galli-Curci.'

'Where's she come fae?'

'Italy.'

Plainly, Elsie was disappointed. 'I don't like Italian film-stars. They're a' too big in the boobs.'

'Yes.'

'I mean, whi' *American* film-star dae a remind you o'?'

'I can't think of anyone.'

'Oh, thanks very much! Hiv you any idea how much this mascara cost me?'

'Not enough, or you would have used less.'

Again I saw that surprised and appreciative glint in her eyes before she laughed. 'That's quite good, that. Cheeky bugger! Of course, it's all right for you. You're well-aff. So yer mate tell't Ada. But A knew that right away.'

'I'm a fourth-year apprentice – if you call that "well-off"!'

'Aye. But yer family's got money. That's how I'm hingin' in wi' ye.'

'Oh.'

She clicked her tongue in annoyance, thinking she'd offended me. 'That's a joke. At least, ye're meant tae *take* it as a joke.'

'I see.'

The proprietor emerged from the store-room and I asked him for tea and Elsie's firm preference of orange Club biscuits.

'Ye're no' very sharp, are ye, Billy? Still, A suppose you've never hid tae be. Ye'd starve fur want o' a shout in oor hoose.'

'What about your family?'

'They can look after theirsels.'

'Are there many of you?'

'Six weans an' me. I'm the eldest.'

'Seven!'

'At the last count,' she grinned. 'But hell, wi' ma Maw ye never know the minute.'

'And your father . . . is he . . . ?'

She gave a yelp. 'Oh! It's him that dis it, all right!'

'What does he work at, though?'

'Whi' *is* this, an examination?'

'I'm sorry. I'll go and get the tea.'

'Sit on yer erse! Jist gie him a shout an' he'll bring it ower.'

'No. I want to . . . ask him something.'

'Suit yersel. Whit's the record?'

I'd hoped she wouldn't notice that. But, anyway, I managed to smuggle it to the counter without further question. I'd already arranged with the proprietor to have it played and he accepted it without surprise. There weren't many people in the cafe and none of them looked down-right anti-operatic. I returned to the table with the tea and biscuits.

Elsie was worried about her appointment with Curt Jürgens. 'Whi' time is it?'

'We've got plenty of time.'

'Fur whit?'

'To get to know each other.'

Elsie loudly snapped her Club biscuit in half before she removed the foil, 'Aw, is that whi' we're daein'? Gettin' tae know each other wi' a table between us?'

The background music now moved perceptibly into the foreground and we heard a soaring soprano voice in a bravura piece full of dramatic leaps and staccato repetitions. I brought the sound to Elsie's attention. 'Listen!'

'What?'

'Listen to her voice. Could you do that?'

'That's no' singin' – that screechin',' was Elsie's opinion, but she listened and upon one of the more intricate and testing repetitions she joined in – making a credible duet of the solo record. It was astonishing to hear that achingly pure sound come from that snub-nose, tiny girl with frizzy red hair leaning casually back from the cafe table. On one hearing she followed the piece, note for intricately pitched note as they tumbled after each other at dazzling speed. When the duet was over all the people in the cafe joined me in applauding Elsie.

'Marvellous!' I cried.

Elsie nodded – pleased with herself, now that I was pleased – and asked, 'Who was that singin'?'

'*That* was Galli-Curci! And *you* are amazing!'

'I was only imitatin' her.'

'Yes, I know. But, don't you see – you *could*! You heard it once and you followed her perfectly. That is amazing.'

'Aye, but what good is it? Ye cannae rock an' roll tae that kinda stuff. Ye couldnae even get intae a skiffle group.'

Then, and on other occasions, I did point out to her that successful opera singers make a lot of money. She conceded that maybe they did – but nobody ever heard of them; an assertion which would have caused Madame Callas a twinge, since she was then at the height of her powers. But I could see the point. Nobody that Elsie knew had ever heard of Maria Callas.

Frank hadn't heard of her either, but he was fascinated by my interest in Elsie. Early that summer – which was to prove one of the sunniest on record – we took our bikes on the ferry across to Kilcreggan from where we started the ritual circuit of The Three Lochs. I was glad to get away from my digs and Frank was glad to have a cycling companion not nearly as fit as himself.

We arrived back at the pier as the gloaming started to slip into darkness and the scanning beam of the Cloch Lighthouse was bright enough to make the sweat on our faces shine as it swept the shore at unvarying intervals. Frank returned to the subject of promoting Elsie's ability.

'Suppose ye do get somebody tae listen tae her . . .' He threw a pebble far out into the water and paused to hear the effect before continuing; ' . . . y'know, somebody that would allow her tae get on . . . She'd hiv tae go away, wouldn't she?'

'Mmm,' I agreed.

He bent down to find another suitable pebble. 'Tae London, or abroad, maybe?'

'Probably.'

'Well . . . if . . .' He threw again with even greater effort. 'If she was away – whit good wid that be tae you?'

'I'd be very pleased.'

'Aye – but she widnae bother aboot ye then.'

'She doesn't bother about me now! I wish she would.'

'Dae ye?' There was a new, more alert note of interest in his voice.

'Of course. I wish she'd take my advice and make some effort to . . . '

'Aw . . . that! I thought maybe ye were serious aboot her.'

'I *am* serious. She has a marvellous voice.'

'Aye. But her voice is no' *her*, is it?' The alertness was gone and now there was some impatience. 'How are ye gettin' on wi' *her*?'

'What do you mean?'

Frank's words picked very decorously at what he saw as the situation. 'She thinks you're too . . . shy. So Ada says.'

'How are you and Ada getting on?'

'All right.' He altered his pitching position for a 'skimmer'. 'Sort a . . . steady . . . y'know. She's quite a nice lassie, but . . . '

'But, what?'

'She hasnae got much life in her.'

'That's what I thought. But Elsie has plenty of spirit.'

'She has that! Dae you no' *care*?'

'Care?'

'Aboot anybody? I mean . . . personally!'

'Yes.'

'You hivnae any idea whi' A'm talkin' aboot.'

'I don't think you realise how rare Elsie is.'

'A know. A know, A know! She's got "perfect pitch" – whatever that is. Or so you say.'

There was silence for a few minutes during which the Cloch scanned us with its brightening beam. I tried to think of some way to explain the remarkable nature of Elsie's ability. I tugged at Frank's singlet and pointed. 'Do you see that can, floating right out there?'

'Where?'

'Wait until the light comes round again. There!'

'I think so.'

'Wait . . . There!'

'I saw it that time. That's quite a distance.'

'Sure. But if you had just the right pebble and you used all your strength – you could throw it that far.'

'Maybe.'

'And if you were very, very accurate, you could hit that can – once.'

'If I could see it.'

'And if you were lucky.'

'So? Whit's a' this aboot?'

'Think!' I got to my feet in the excitement of what seemed a perfect analogy. 'If you had just the right pebble, if you could get all your strength into one throw, if you were amazingly accurate and very lucky – you could hit that can out there. With all that, and if you could see it, you could hit it – once. Compare that to Elsie's voice. She's able to hit that can any time she wants to – dead on, every time. And in the dark.'

For a long moment Frank stood perfectly still, staring out over the water, then in a voice soft with wonder he murmured, 'Christ!' However, the competitive urge quickly reasserted itself. 'I'll bet you couldnae hit that can.'

'No, I couldn't. But I do know it's there.'

'Oh, grandeur, b'Jesus!'

'I do, and I'm prepared to say so.'

He shook his head dismissively. 'You're a funny bloke.'

'So you say.'

'So everybody says – an' a lot mair!'

'Oh?'

'D'ye know what I used tae tell them, when we startit' here?'

'That I was daft.'

'Aye, but apart fae that – I tell't them you've got a bad heart.'

'I haven't.'

'A know! A know, ye havenae. It was jist in case ye got intae a fight – tae make them go easy on ye. In case ye died on them.'

'Thanks a lot.'

'But noo I think there *is* somethin' wrang wi' yer heart.'

'Oh?'

'Whit dae ye call they things musicians use – that wag fae side tae side?'

'A metronome.'

'That's it! That's whit you've got, tickin' away in yer chist.'

'I'm sorry you think so.'

'So am A, pal. So am A.'

Now that Frank was converted on the value of 'perfect pitch', he convinced Elsie. Since he was not a fanciful outsider who just happened to be passing through, she believed him. We called a joint meeting of four in the cafe to hammer out what should be done.

'There must be somewhere she could go,' Frank said. 'Tae start wi', at least. Is there no' any night-school for singers, or anything like that?'

'A don't want tae go tae night-school,' Elsie stated.

Ada was morosely philosophical. 'Ye've got tae start somewhere, Elsie.'

I shook my head. 'There's only musical appreciation classes. What Elsie should have is training.'

'Where?'

'There's the Academy of Music in Glasgow,' I suggested. 'We could write to them and see what they say.'

That was too indecisive for Frank. 'Don't bother writin'. You an' Elsie go up and see them.'

'If we did that they'd probably want to hear an audition piece.'

'A whit?' asked Elsie.

'They'd want to hear you sing pieces from opera.'

'But a' they songs is in a foreign language!'

Ada was appalled. 'Oh, God! Ye hiv tae learn a foreign language next.' I was beginning to doubt the usefulness of Ada at this meeting.

'No,' I said firmly. 'She doesn't.'

Frank was glad to take up my denial. 'Naw, she doesnae, ya stupit bitch.' But he gave me a worried, enquiring, look to discover why this should be so.

'You can learn the words without learning the language. As long as you know what they mean.'

'Right!' said Frank. 'There must be a teacher in Greenock that could learn ye a coupla songs. So – that's the first thing. Eh, Bill?'

'Yes.'

'Ada! Run oot an' get us the night's paper.'

'Och!'

'Go on! We hiv tae look up the adver*tise*ments.'

We watched Ada as though the world was waiting for her to leave in search of the local newspaper. And she took her time about it, fiddling with this and that before she even scraped back her chair. She knew it was the most attention *she* was going to get all night. When she'd gone, I tried to establish other possibilities of advancement.

'What do your parents suggest?' I asked Elsie.

'Nothin'. I havenae tell't them.'

'Why not?'

'Whit could they dae?'

'She's right,' said Frank. 'An' they might try an' stop her.'

'Surely not! They must be interested in . . .'

'Naw!'

'Never!'

They adopted identical expressions, shaking their heads slowly and smiling tolerantly at my naive assumption.

'They've got enough tae think aboot,' was Elsie's summary. 'They don't need me tae cause any mair bother. As long as A'm workin' they'll be quite happy.'

Frank nodded. 'Sure thing. She's got tae keep her job while she's daein' this trainin', ye know!'

'I don't think that would be possible.'

'Then ye kin forget it!' said Elsie flatly.

We all looked down at our empty cups and at the little mound of coloured foil from a good half-dozen orange Club biscuits. At that moment I felt like forgetting it. Around me, I became aware of the murmured conversations of other people in the cafe for whom a dream was not, so suddenly, evaporating. And behind that murmur, supporting them, was the discreet music of a Gilbert & Sullivan favourite in an orchestral version. To me it was incomprehensible that Elsie's parents and friends, not to mention

Elsie herself, could so misjudge what should have been the order of priorities. I glanced across to Frank for help in this embarrassing situation. And he came through. 'Here! Wait a minute. Is there no' Grants or Scholarships?'

I jumped at the idea. 'Yes! Of course there are. I'm practically sure there are.'

'Ye see, Elsie, they wid pay ye money while ye were trainin'.'

'Fur singin'?'

'Aye!'

'Then they should hiv their heids looked,' was Elsie's opinion.

'That's something we could ask about at the Academy.'

Ada, apparently exhausted, walked towards us carrying the Telegraph. She explained, 'A had tae wait for the fella comin' oot o' a pub. But there ye are!' She threw it down on the table where it was immediately seized by Frank.

He asked, 'How much dae ye think a singin' teacher wid take fur a coupla songs?'

'That would depend on how long it took Elsie to learn them.'

Elsie brightened a little. 'A widnae take long. Y'know, maybe if A wis singin' in a foreign language, A widnae sound like a wee scrubber.'

'Right!' Ada said. 'Maybe that's how a' they other singers dae it.'

Elsie laughed. 'Is that right, Bill? Whi' aboot that wan A wis imitatin'? Wis she a wee scrubber?'

I gasped at the accuracy of this. 'Yes! As a matter of fact, she was – about sixty years ago, in Milan.'

'Well, there's hope fur me yet.'

It was at that moment the splendid idea occurred to me which was to have so much importance in our plan. 'Yes! Yes! And she's still alive!'

'Whit's up?' Frank was startled at my vehemence.

'Madame Galli-Curci is still alive! In her late seventies, she must be – but she's still alive.'

'So what?'

'We could record Elsie's voice on a tape and send it to her. She lives in America. California, I think. We could send her the tape and ask for her help. If *she* liked it everybody would listen to her opinion. She could lift Elsie right out of this place; in the same way that she was lifted out of the slums in Milan.'

Ada saw the justice in that. 'Noo she's really famous, this woman, is she?'

'Yes! Oh yes, she is. And she must still remember how difficult it was when she was starting.'

Frank wasn't so sure. 'She must get hundreds of people askin' her tae speak for them.'

'I expect so. But how many have the quality Elsie has? This isn't just another person asking for help; it's somebody who deserves it.'

Elsie punched my shoulder. 'I wish A wis as sure as you are.'

Frank quickly returned his attention to the small ads., but I knew he was about to latch onto the next positive step. 'There's a place in Glasgow where ye can make records,' he said, without looking up. 'But that'll cost money as well. An' if ye're gonnae make a job o' it, you'll need tae learn the songs. There's a wumman here that might dae.' He slid the paper towards me.

'How much does she charge?' Elsie wanted to know.

'Not very much.'

'Good. 'Cause a hivnae got very much.'

'Who has?' observed Ada.

'Aye,' Frank said, 'the money's another thing we've got tae think aboot. Maybe we could hiv a whip-roon some o' your mates, Elsie. Hauf o' them must be on the gemme.'

'Are they hell! They a' dae it fur nothin'.'

'A don't dae it at a'!' Ada protested. 'Don't you call me a hooer.'

'Wish A could,' growled Frank.

'Aw – poor fella!'

It bothered me a little that they could joke about raising money but I tried to sound reassuring. 'I'm sure we could raise enough for a few lessons and for the recording.'

Even the assurance that the money could be raised was enough for Frank. 'Right! First, the lessons. We'll go and see this wumman.'

'Now?'

'Aye, "Now"! But no' you. If this teacher heard you talkin' she might double her price for a kick-aff.'

'True enough,' said Elsie. 'Me an' Frank'll go. You jist write doon the songs ye want me tae learn. Here, write it on the bottom o' the paper.'

Frank grunted. 'Oh, naw! Bill's got a notebook. Haven't ye, son? Bugger never moves withoot his notebook.'

'Whit does he cairry a notebook fur?' whispered Ada.

Frank whispered back, 'Tae prove he's livin'.'

I tore out the page on which I'd listed three arias. 'There you are. Tell her these are just suggestions.'

Elsie and Frank set off immediately and I was left with the dolorous Ada to our mutual unease and silence. 'Well,' I said at last, 'I'd better get back to my digs.'

'Who is it ye're ludgin' wi?'

'A family called Mulvenny.'

'Is it nice?'

'Not very. The husband's an invalid, so I have to do all the odd jobs around the house.' Silence fell again. 'Well – I'd better go.'

'So ye said.'

'Yes.'

'That wumman in America . . . ?'

'Galli-Curci!'

'Did she get mairrit'?'

'I don't know. Does it matter?'

'It wid ma'er tae Elsie. Aw she talks aboot is gettin' mairrit an' havin' a squaad o' weans.'

The next few weeks leading up to the Fair holidays were devoted to activities aimed at promoting Elsie. There were rehearsals of her audition pieces; bus journeys to Glasgow in search of records by other singers and, on the way home, a crash-course in operatic plots. Elsie seemed to enjoy those top-deck viva voce examinations as assorted drunks on *their* way home kept up an interminable serenade.

'Tell me about Gilda,' I prompted.

'Gilda. Gilda is the hunchback's daughter. The hunchback wants the other man tae kill the Duke. But the daughter fancies the Duke . . . so . . . she gets dressed up as a man and walks right in tae get knifed. Then they put her in a bag – bleedin' like a pig, but still alive. Then they gie the bag tae the hunchback and, er . . . ' The laughter she'd been fighting to suppress burst through. She struggled to resume. 'They gie this bag wi' Gilda in it tae the hunchback . . . *and* . . . he's no' very pleased. They let her oot the bag tae sing, but then she dies.'

Much as she liked the plot of *Rigoletto*, she found *Tosca* even more hilarious. Indeed, she was quick to discover a basic lack of savvy – or even common sense – in the behaviour of people in opera. 'They seem determined tae get kill't,' she said. 'Especially the weemin!' I explained to her that these were tragedies. She wouldn't accept it. Anything as unnecessary and basically funny as *Tosca*, she thought, couldn't become a tragedy just by calling it that. 'Who,' she wanted to know, 'dae they think they're kiddin'?' She saw much more sense in 'real fantasy' because everybody knows it *is* fantasy, and she became quite attached to the story of Olympia in *The Tales of Hoffmann*. That was what she concentrated on in the few more singing lessons that could be afforded. As the weeks went by, Frank became more and more impatient. One morning, as he scorched away at the grinder in the Fitting Shop, he told me. 'She'll no' dae it any better than she's daein' it. Make her an appointment.' So – I wrote to the Academy of Music in Glasgow.

Elsie and I took the afternoon off. It was a Thursday. The weather was hot and sticky. The bus was crammed and we were crushed against the window on the long upper-deck seat; Elsie trying to keep her sheets of music flat and I trying to avoid leg-cramp by using the jolts to alter position.

Very gradually, the Clyde narrowed, darkened, then disappeared among the docks and grimy warehouses of the city. The current of nervousness grew between us and that charged all the latent doubts we'd had about this odd enterprise. Swaying through the grim streets under the glare of that sunlight, our assurance oozed away. It just did not seem possible that a world-famed career in opera could begin this way. And yet, if it did, how satisfying success would be. From the Rope Works to Covent Garden. If Galli-Curci could do it in Milan why couldn't Elsie do it in Glasgow, fifty years of progress later?

I glanced at Elsie; her make-up already in need of repair, wearing an over-elaborate dress she'd bought to be a bridesmaid some time ago. But her voice, I kept telling myself; they must recognise what a marvellous voice she has.

Eventually, after two mistaken changes of bus and a long exhausting trek up Buchanan Street, we presented ourselves at the desk of the Academy of Music. And for the entire interview we stood, right there at the desk. No, they did not want to hear her sing. No, they did not think there would be any point in seeing anyone else. No, scholarships were not awarded to outsiders. No, she could not become a student without passing an examination which would show she had reached the academic standard required. 'Good afternoon,' and we were out on the dusty pavement again.

Elsie grinned. 'They certainly know what they *don't* want, eh?'

'I'm sorry.'

'Don't you worry aboot it, Billy. You did your best fur me, and that's that.'

'No!'

'You heard whi' the man tell't ye! They only want well-educated singers that don't hiv tae earn a livin'.'

'To hell with them!'

'Good fur you! That's whi' A think. If A wis well-educated an' didnae hivtae earn a livin' A'm damned sure A widnae go near that place. They've nae bloody chairs, for a start!'

We both laughed. 'So it seems. But you're still going to make that recording. Today. If only we can find someone to accompany you.'

'Whi' fur? A can sing they songs withoot a piana.'

I grasped that defiant little figure in pink chiffon by the arms and whirled her round, cutting a clear circle in the flow of the sweating pedestrians. 'Of course! Of course you can. All right! We'll record it and send it off today. Since that stuffy lot wouldn't have you, we'll send a gift to Galli-Curci!'

'And has she replied?' asked my mother.

'Not yet. But that was only a few days before I came down here.' I was spending a week of my holidays with my parents in Sussex and told my mother the story as I followed her round the garden.

'I'd no idea Galli-Curci was still alive. We saw her in New York when I was a girl.'

'What was she in?'

'Probably *Traviata*. She did that a good deal. She never sang in England, though. I can't think why.'

'Perhaps she wasn't well enough educated.'

'What, darling?'

'Nothing.'

My mother did not pursue it and, for a few moments, gave most of her attention to flower selection. On the garden path in the warm sunlight we seemed to be wading in a sluggish stream of perfume which was stirred and lifted by our movement. My mother added, 'Her most famous role was Gilda in *Rigoletto*.'

'Elsie would be a perfect Gilda, though she might refuse to die in a sack.'

'I wish you'd brought the recording down with you, instead of sending it off to California.'

'It was important to send it that day.'

'Why?'

'To make up for a disappointment.'

'Ah, yes.' She did not pursue that either. My mother had a great knack of gracefully minding her own business.

'Isn't there anyone you could interest in hearing her?'

'I don't know.'

'Would you try to think of someone?'

'This afternoon?'

'All we need is a well-known musician whose opinion is respected.'

'Aren't there any respected opinions in Scotland?'

'Only on education. We need somebody in opera. What about all those parties you go to – and the fund-raising? You must know hundreds of suitable people.'

'Less than a hundred and I'd know far fewer if I kept thrusting aspiring Gildas at them.'

'I'm not asking you to keep on doing it. I'm asking you to do it once, for one girl.' It seemed to me the pace of this conversation was far too slow and detached. Now it stopped entirely in another foray of snipping.

'She must be a remarkable girl,' said the lady, a little too evenly to be entirely casual.'

'She is!'

'Then why hasn't she made some effort on her own behalf?'

'Because she's only sixteen and she's too busy helping to feed her many brothers and sisters.'

'I'm sorry. That was a foolish question.'

'It was, rather. You've no idea how they live. And nobody cares.'

'Except you,' said my mother, smiling to herself. Then she conjured up a name. 'Eric Delber!'

'What?'

'The conductor – Eric Delber. He's doing a tour, including Scotland.'

'When?'

'Ah . . . When did he tell me it was? Or maybe it's over.'

'How can we find out?'

'I'll call his wife.'

'Now!'

'No – when I have filled this basket. You realise, of course, that I would have to hear her before I could recommend her to Eric.'

'Oh! I don't think she could manage to come down here.'

'Of course not. I've been promising to visit Mrs Mulvenny again. Perhaps she'd let me use her piano to hear Elsie sing.'

'That wouldn't be a good idea – I mean, coming to the Mulvennys. Mr Mulvenny is at home now.'

'Ah!' She did not want to know why that was a deterrent. 'Well, no doubt we'll be able to manage somewhere else.'

We'd been back at work a couple of weeks when I burst upon Frank in the millwright's 'howf' where he was doing a rush 'home-job'; hammering away at an immovable gas valve as though his life depended on it. I had to shout for

154

him to notice me at all. 'Frank! Frank, stop that for a minute!'

He continued hammering and shouted over the noise, 'Whit's up?'

'Look!' I brandished the letter under his nose.

'Whit's that?'

'A letter from California. I got it this morning.'

'Whi' does she say?'

'It's from her secretary. It says, "Dear Mr Thompson, Madame Galli-Curci thanks you for your gift."'

'And . . . ? Whi' else?'

'That's it. "Madame Galli-Curci thanks you for your gift," and nothing else at all.'

'Christ! She's got a hard neck.'

'Maybe she didn't understand what I wanted her to do. But I did explain.'

'Aye. She understood all right.' He started slapping the head of the hammer against his palm and I could feel his anger building up.

'Or maybe she's forgotten what it felt like to be in Elsie's position.'

'Naw!' He dealt a blow against the jammed valve which rocked the vice. 'Mair likely she disnae want tae remember. There's nane wi' a hazier idea o' poverty than them that's got by it.'

'I don't believe that.'

'You! Whi' the hell dae you know aboot poverty?' He was perfectly willing to seize on anything as a source of irritation.

'And I don't believe she even saw the letter. It must have gone straight to her secretary and she sent a stock reply.'

'Either way, it wulnae dae Elsie any good.' He started on an accelerating barrage of hammer blows which turned the rest of our exchange into more of a shouting-match than a conversation. 'An' whit's worse . . . ye've spent money . . . on a present . . . tae a wumman that disnae need it . . . an' disnae want it!'

'We agreed! It was worth a try.'

'It wis your idea.'

155

'Maybe . . . Frank! Maybe Eric Delber will do something for her.'

'Oh! Maybe he will. Maybe the Academy will take her on. Maybe an auld wumman in America'll wave a magic wand. Maybe she could win a scholarship.' He paused from sheer physical exhaustion of hammering to shout into my face. 'Ye're full o' fuckin' maybees, an' ye've got that wee lassie's heid wastit'.' I stared at him with my mouth open. I'd seen him angry before but never as now, vulnerable to the anger. Something in my expression must have taken the heat out of the moment for he went on in a curiously sad and flat voice, 'Maybe it's jist no' worth a' the bother.'

Eric Delber's tour included a week in Glasgow. My mother came up a few days earlier and booked a room in the hotel where the conductor was staying. That Saturday was Elsie's birthday and I took her to Glasgow for tea. It was agreed we would meet my mother in the lounge at three-thirty to have a chat first. When we eventually arrived mother signalled the waiter at once, then extended her hand to us. 'Darling! I was beginning to give up hope.'

'The bus was waylaid by a crowd going to a football match.'

'And you are Elsie! I'm delighted to meet you.'

'How do you do, Mrs Thompson.'

'Sit beside me, my dear.'

As Elsie settled herself on the sofa, as though preparing for a siege, I further explained our delay. 'They all wanted to get on our bus, but the conductress wouldn't budge with more than five standing inside. There was quite an argument.'

'Surely they could count to five!'

'Yes. It was a question of *which* five.'

'A right bunch o' neds!' Elsie reported.

Mother smiled in agreement and touched Elsie delicately at the wrist. 'I do like your coat,' she said; and probably she did. Anyway, Elsie was visibly cheered and the waiter laid the tea things before us. 'How is the family?'

'They're a'right.'

'Good.' She thanked the waiter and seemed preoccupied

arranging the cups while really waiting to see if the girl was going to say anything. Failing that, she went on, 'There's a music room here they will let us have the use of. I hope I can do you justice, Elsie.'

'Pardon me?'

'In the accompaniment,' mother explained.

'Dae you play the piana!'

'Yes; though not as well as I used to. Oh, Bill!'

'Mm?'

'I've forgotten to bring down the music – would you get it?' She handed me the key to her room.

'Where did you leave it?'

'I can't remember that either. Just look around and you'll find it.'

'Excuse me,' I said, and left them side by side. It was not until a long time later that my mother felt willing to give a report on that conversation.

Elsie had immediately decided she would have to make *some* contribution. 'It's very nice o' ye tae come a' this way tae hear me.'

'Well – it wasn't only to hear you. I've been promising for a long time to visit Bill's landlady and I did also want to hear the programme Mr Delber is presenting in Glasgow.'

'That's good.'

'Do you know it?'   .

'Naw. A mean, at least ye'll get somethin' oot o' the journey.'

'You're being far too modest. Bill has a very good ear and he says you're wonderful.'

'Maybe that's jist whi' he wants tae believe.'

'I'm sorry?' Mother was having difficulty coping with Elsie's unfenced vowels, as well as her imperviousness to flattery.

'Bill's a nice fella, but he's awfa easy takin' in.'

'Is he?'

'Dae *you* no' think so?'

'Probably I do think so, but I'm not sure that I understand you.'

'He's a bit up in the air, y'know?'

'Yes, he is!' She was relieved at getting that bit. 'And you are not.'

'Me? Naw! That's no' ma style at a'.'

'I'm glad to hear it.'

'For ma sake, or his?'

The pertinence of this question threw mother for a moment, but she was getting into the swing of the very direct approach. 'Well . . . for both your sakes.'

'Ye don't hiv tae worry aboot that.'

'About what?'

'Aboot whi' was worryin' ye.'

Again she had scored a bull's-eye and they busied themselves with the tea in silence while mother came to terms with this very practical woman who'd just turned seventeen. She began, 'You're a very astu . . . You're a very clever girl, Elsie.'

'Well – A didnae come up the Clyde in a barra'. An' *you* didnae forget tae bring doon yer music.'

Mother laughed. 'That's true!' She realised that she was actually enjoying this conversation.

'No' that A don't fancy him, mind ye. But when he looks at me a' he sees is a coupla tonsils jiggin' aboot.'

'Oh, come now! I don't think that's quite fair.'

'It's *no'* fair. But it's true. He disnae seem me at a'.'

'Then he's missing quite a lot.'

'Naw! He'll never miss whi' he never wantit'.'

'But he does want you to be recognised and valued for your ability.'

'Sure! A know. So, A'd better be good, eh?'

And she was. My mother was certainly impressed enough to recommend her to Eric Delber who saw Elsie, alone, the following day. It was a relief that, now, other people were doing things and I was very glad to let them get on with it. If Elsie was going to make any headway, I couldn't always be there. So, it was mother who went backstage after the concert to hear Mr Delber's opinion.

'Eric!'

'Marianne! My dear, how sweet of you to come round.'

'Congratulations! It was a wonderful performance.'

'Thank you. And the audience was much better, too. Of course, they have a good Ear, Nose and Throat hospital in Glasgow.'

'What do you mean?'

'A Glasgow audience will always hear, rarely sneeze and cough only when it is absolutely necessary.' They laughed together. Delber set up another wine-glass and offered to pour. 'Will you have some of this?'

'Yes, thank you. Then I can drink to your success.'

'Oh, no! We will drink to *your* success.'

'Mine?'

'Yes. To your discovery. I heard her sing today. I couldn't understand a word she said, but when she sang . . . !'

'I am glad you liked her.'

'I'm going to call Chicago when I get back to the hotel.'

'Chicago!'

'The opera-school there. I have a roving commission from them to find a coloratura. Well – I've found her. Or, rather, you found her for me. And she's young enough to take the full training. They'll be delighted about that. Should be ready for the '62/'63 season.'

'I'm so glad that something can be done.'

'And she seems a very level-headed girl. Quite . . . resilient . . . really.' The word he'd thought of was 'tough,' as they both knew.

My mother came instantly to her defence. 'I suppose she's had to be. But with three years' training, I wonder how her family will manage.'

'You needn't worry about that. She and her family will be very well taken care of and provided for. Let me give you a lift back to the hotel. My car's waiting.'

'Thank you. I really am most grateful to you, Eric.'

'It's Chicago and I who are grateful to you. I think we and you and all of opera can look forward to Elsie's career with great satisfaction.'

From then on everything was taken entirely out of my hands. Delber had made a recording of his own to send to Chicago. They responded as enthusiastically as a cable would allow. Or so Delber's wife told my mother, who sent me a note. Elsie herself seemed to be avoiding me so I had no idea how closely they kept her informed of progress, but around the middle of September it was settled that Elsie would make a preliminary visit to Chicago for final approval and signing the contract. About that time, too, Frank suggested that we make a last-of-the-year circuit of the Three Lochs. It wasn't a successful outing. Most of the time he just grunted at my questions. He seemed anxious to keep going, so we reached the final stretch much earlier than usual. But that long steep hill over the back of the Roseneath peninsula was too much for me.

'Frank!'

'Save yer breath!' he shouted from several yards ahead, pedalling strong.

'I've got to stop!' I gasped and just tumbled off at the roadside.

He kept going. 'We're nearly there!'

'I've got to take a rest.'

He glanced back then practically stood his bike on end as he whipped an about-turn. As he free-wheeled down to me he shouted with that edge of impatience he'd been displaying all day. 'Whi's the matter wi' ye? We're nearly at the crest.'

'What's the matter with *you*?'

'A could've made it if A wis masel'.'

'You might as well have been,' I told him, controlling my breath with painful difficulty.

'Whi' that?'

'You've been acting as though I weren't with you. Sit down for a minute.'

A car passed us, grinding slowly up the hill in second gear and for a moment polluting the clear scent of early Autumn with fumes of unburned petrol. Aided by overcoming the sound of the engine, Frank was able to shout – accomplishing an even quicker than usual transition from impatience to anger, 'Christ Almighty! It's no' a picnic.'

'Frank!'

' "Frank!" ' he mimicked. 'Jesus! Aw, away an' pick some heather.' He slumped down beside me on the grass verge. I waited and he went on, more quietly, 'What? What d'ye want me tae say?'

'Whatever it is that you've been trying not to say.'

He gave me a hard, cold look and did exactly that. 'Right! Elsie and me is goin' tae get mairrit.'

'Oh!' That was nowhere near what I expected him to say. 'When she comes back, you mean?'

'Naw! Next month, A mean.' He paused. 'She asked me tae tell ye.'

'But what good will that do? She'll be in America for three years.'

'She's no goin' tae America. At all! She'll no sign the contract. She'll stay right where she is.'

'Oh!' An area of coldness was beginning to expand in my stomach and I became acutely aware of the coarse texture of the grass stubble under my fingers. 'Why?' I asked him.

'Because she wants tae get mairrit! Tae me!'

I recalled Ada's words. ' "An' hiv a squaad o' weans"?'

'Likely! She'll hiv wan anyway – in the spring.'

'Oh.'

'For God's sake! Will ye stop saying, "Oh"!'

'But everything has been arranged for her. Does she really want to get married?'

'Aye. That's whi' she wants. That's whi' she's always wantit. She's no' a bloody puppet, y'know, that can be wound up tae dae whi' you an' yer fancy freens want.'

'But she'll do what you want?'

'I want tae marry her. That's different. And there's another thing A've tae tell ye . . . *ask* ye.'

'What?'

'A'd like you tae be ma best man.'

'Why?'

'Whit dae ye mean, "Why"? Because you're ma mate – an' ye know how tae dae things right. Will ye?'

'Yes,' I said, wondering a little how I could be both a source of irritation and a pillar of support. 'I'd like to.'

'Great!' He sprang to his feet, smiling for the first time that day. 'You've been a good pal tae me, Billy. An' ye certainly picked me a winner. Noo, come on!' He raised his bike and set it on the road with one hand. 'I'll race ye doon

161

tae the boat.' Relieved of the burden, he pulled strongly away – up the last yards of the hill. He disappeared over the crest with a triumphant wave of his arm.

All that was twenty-five years ago. A year after Elsie's first baby was born – and while she was carrying her second – I finished my time and went to sea. Frank, having done his home service, went off to do his National Service. I never heard from them again and never forgave them for that loss and that waste of talent. But I do hope they've been happy. To deprive us of another Galli-Curci, the least they owe us is to be happy. Oddly enough, Madame Galli-Curci died in 1963 – the very year that Elsie would have made her debut. Shortly after that, the tape we had sent to California was returned to me. I have it still. Elsie singing Olympia's 'List' To the Song Of My Heart' – the plea of the fabulous doll in *The Tales of Hoffmann*. I have her voice, but Elsie, herself, was never the sort of girl to be turned into a puppet; no matter how beautifully it may sing.

Lord Sweatrag

My final year was spent in the Drawing Office among the soft-talking, paper-rustling elite of the shipyard where I learned to fashion the ultimate and perfect 4H chisel-edge pencil, capable – if used – of making the very whisper of a line which had direction but no thickness. A line capable of transporting any female tracer to a distraction of delight and possibly an eye-specialist. There, too, I found the solution to a mystery which had previously baffled me and my colleagues on the shop-floor for many months. It was the secret cause of the bitter feud between a senior apprentice, Jock Turnbull and the labourer, Lord Sweatrag. The whole affair was inexplicable. Lord Sweatrag's action, which had been such a bizarre starting point in the middle of the Heavy Turning bay, the mysterious and secret management discussions that had followed it and then the weird change in Jock's behaviour were all connected – but how? It seemed entirely apt that, like so much information desperately required by 'the shops', the Drawing Office kept the facts to itself. On my first day there I learned more about the strange labourer than I'd managed to gather in the four years when I'd seen him practically every day.

He was called Lord Sweatrag in recognition of his taciturn, aristocratic manner and his domination of the sweat-rag trade. A sweat-rag was a nine-inch square of loose-woven stringy cloth used for wiping muck off the hands and never, to my knowledge, sweat off the brow. I have no idea, now, why they were so fiercely coveted, but I did not question it at the time. Initially we were issued with two clean rags every Wednesday *if* we could hand in two dirty

163

ones. Given lucky finds, seniority or theft, that number could be increased. Theft was simple because custom dictated that the sweat-rag was worn, not in, but hanging out of the right-hand trouser pocket. However you came by them, you got back exactly the number you offered. Lord Sweatrag was adamant about that. He had a little single-entry cash book in which were listed all our names and with the L. s. d. columns converted to note: 'Lifted', 'Supplied' and 'Date'. After my first couple of weeks I tried to make friends with this odd man that all my workmates sneered at.

'How many?' he asked, standing at the other side of my machine, account book at the ready.

'Two,' I said.

'Still only two?' He made the appropriate note in his book.

I didn't know if he was deriding my lack of enterprise or commending my honesty. And I didn't know what to call him. All I'd been told was, this is Lord Sweatrag and he's a loony. He deposited the soiled rags at the front end of his barrow and lifted two clean ones from the back. Before handing them over, one by one, he snapped them in the way shopkeepers used to snap the old five-pound notes.

'There you are. One . . . and . . . one.'

'Thank you, Mr . . . er . . . '

'What?'

'I've forgotten your name.'

'It's Chinese,' he said, without a smile. 'Hey-You!'

I laughed. 'Yes. But what's your English name?'

'My Scottish name is Dalziel.'

'Sorry.'

'There's no need to apologise to me,' he said, and moved his barrow on to the next machine.

He was, then, a man in his mid-fifties, thin, with a military bearing and a razor-edge parting in his sleeked-down grey hair. He'd been in the Army – a Quartermaster Sergeant, I'd been told. The charge of being a loony seemed to arise from nothing more than his attitude to his work. He treated the filthy, menial job of labourer with the fastidious care of an exacting professional. There was also the fact he didn't like people, but I could see nothing loony about that. More suspect, in my view, was his obsessive interest in the Drawing Office. He desperately wanted to work there among 'the gentlemen at boards' as he always called the draughtsmen. The fact that, as a matter of course, I would finish my time there was enough for him to treat me with special interest.

I never did manage to acquire more than the regulation two sweat-rags and that seemed to please him. He placed great trust in regulations, but none at all in his fellow man. And he saw everything that was going on. Often when there was some upset or accident – or even argument – the one person not moving or shouting or perturbed would be Lord Sweatrag. He would stand an even distance away, almost at attention, his shrewd, unblinking eyes taking in every detail. When I was in imminent danger of being greased it was he who suddenly materialised and thwarted the attempt. By then we were on speaking terms. That had come about because of a book I was reading at lunch-time. A shadow fell on the page and I looked up to find him poised over me.

'What are you reading?' he asked. It was meant to be conversational but, with his lack of practice, it came out a shade peremptory.

I lifted the book to show him. '*The Republic*. Plato.'

'Why?'

'Pardon?'

'Are you reading it because it's a fine book to be caught reading, or because you want to find out if he agrees with you?' This question was delivered literally over my head, but then he gave a quick downward glance which warned me that it might be a trick question. I gave the matter a little thought. The pause did not please him. 'If you're as unsure as that you could have saved the Greenock Public Library the bother of getting it for you.'

I said, 'I'm reading it because other writers, that I've enjoyed reading, speak highly of it.'

He raised his eye-brows wearily. 'And don't you think they might speak highly of it for one of the two reasons I put to *you*?'

'I hadn't thought of that.'

165

'Even writers you enjoy reading have their vanities.'

'Have you read it?' I asked.

'Good,' he said and raised his hand to give my question a one-finger salute. 'Good. A knight's move question.'

'How is that?' It occurred to me that he may have rehearsed all this before he approached me. On the other hand, it could be that I was just slow on the uptake.

'You've dodged one square to the side of the two squares I put in line – which places you in a good position to attack, whatever I say.'

'And what do you say?'

'I say, yes, I have read *The Republic*. And I made notes on it. I always made notes on any serious books I was reading. Do you keep notebooks?'

'No.'

'You should. You'll never be young again. This is the most important time to remember. Your training. Accuracy. Have something certain in your life – even if it's past.'

'I have my class notebooks.'

'I'm not talking about that. No, no. It's not the academic stuff that's important. What I mean is organisation, records, planning. That's the sort of thing they'll want in the Drawing Office.'

'Do you keep records like that?'

'Certainly. I can tell you to a penny how much I spent in any week five years ago – *and* all the comings and goings of the people I was working with.'

'But what use is it?'

'I'll tell you. It demonstrates a well-ordered mind.'

'To whom?'

'To whom it may concern,' said Lord Sweatrag severely. 'I showed some of my notebooks to the Chief Draughtsman when I was interviewed for the post of Clerk to the Drawing Office. I could tell he was impressed.'

'It's a shame you didn't get the job.'

'Yes. I'd be better alongside the gentlemen at boards than among this rabble. It would be much more fitting.' He said it as though, fairly soon, he expected God to admit a gross oversight.

'Who did get the job?'

'A foolish old-wifie of a man that happens to be a cousin of the Chief Draughtsman's wife. He will not last long.'

'Surely he'll always be a cousin of the Chief's wife?'

'A cousin aged about sixty is one thing,' said Sweatrag. 'A cousin in his dotage is quite another.'

For the next few years I moved from one department to another 'gaining experience'. But in whatever part of the sprawling Engine Works I stowed my tools I could be sure to see the aloof, alert, figure of Dalziel. I half suspected that he was watching over me, but I suppose he was just watching over everybody. Jock Turnbull, the senior apprentice, had a theory that the enigmatic labourer was really a management spy.

'You watch him,' he said. 'He's got a microphone hidden in the bristles o' his brush.'

'Surely not!'

Jock crossed his heart with wide strokes.

'Why?'

'Well, it's easier than keepin' his *ear* tae the ground.' He laughed, as he often did, at his own joke and it was such a childish, infectious laugh that it would have been churlish not to join in.

'What does he do with the information?' I asked.

'Transmits it tae they other loony bastards in Personnel.'

One of the messiest jobs that labourers performed was cleaning out the machine sumps. Almost all the machines used soluble oil to cool and lubricate the cutting edge against the metal. Driven by a pump, the mixture of oil and water gushed like a jet of milk from the nozzle above the tool and ran down to accumulate in the sump under the machine. Much else accumulated there, too, and over a period of months the stagnant oil, various droppings and debris thickened into a black, evil-smelling, treacle. This had to be swabbed out by hand and emptied into buckets. Whereas any labourer could be told to do the job, in the Heavy Turning bay it was usually Lord Sweatrag whom the Turners preferred. He made such a good job of it. Practically every working day I'd see him, sleeves rolled neatly well above the elbow, kneeling in a semi-circle of buckets behind a lathe, enveloped in a sickening stench.

I remarked to Jock, 'He seems to take a masochistic pleasure in it.'

'Aye.'

'Like T. E. Lawrence cleaning the latrines.'

'Who?' Jock asked.

'Lawrence of Arabia.'

'In Arabia?'

'No. The latrines were in England.'

'Eh!' Jock gave a bellow of laughter. 'That's a helluva journey for a shite.'

I laughed. There were few pieces of information that Jock could not turn into a joke. He was a big, jovial, young man with large brown eyes which shone with a constant gleam of pleased anticipation. It was his task to enlighten me on the art of 'bedding the bearings' on the big Diesel shafts. This he did by letting me watch him do it. There was no question of letting me try for myself. Nor did he tell me what he was doing, nor why. Instead, he reported at length on the appearance, conversation and behaviour of Helen. He was consumingly in love with a girl called Helen. They'd been engaged for almost a year and he wore a heavy-looking gold ring to prove it. When he thought he wasn't being watched he would polish it and, often, when he rested his strong brown hand on the polished surface of the bearing he seemed to be hypnotised by the astonishing fact of that ring; and the fact that Helen was going to marry him. He thought himself a very lucky young man and worried about his luck holding. But she had promised that as soon as he'd finished his time they would marry. Her one condition was that Jock should not go to sea.

'That must have been a hard decision,' I said. Jock, like nearly all the apprentices, lived in the constant anticipation of the freedom and adventure offered by the merchant fleet. The five years in a shipyard was the ransom we were paying for that.

'Aye, it was hard,' he agreed. 'But I had tae give in. She'd made up her mind.'

'Helen must be a very determined girl.'

'She is that.' His voice had a husky catch of admiration. 'An' she'll be the makin' o' me. Christ, A'd kill masel' if she found somebody else before A'm out o' ma time.'

For the first few weeks I worked with him he kept me informed on how fast that time was passing. Then, quite suddenly his manner changed. There were fewer reports on Helen and far fewer jokes. He became moody and preoccupied. He started having fainting fits; 'blackouts' he called them. It was incongruous that such a big, healthy young man should faint. Fortunately, the job required him to sit on a low stool leaning over the shaft bearings – which meant that usually he did not so much fall as slump unconscious. He was always given prompt First Aid but nothing could revive him for at least five or six minutes. He reported that he'd seen his doctor and was given pills but I never saw him take any. In fact he seemed curiously resigned to the whole business. He laughed about it, although there must have been great danger to him if it happened in the street. At work, because it was Jock, everyone tried to save him any embarrassment. And the foreman didn't insist on sending him home because when eventually he regained consciousness he was perfectly all right and it was known he needed the bonus for the new house. I wondered if he did. It seemed to me likely that the cause of these 'blackouts' was trouble with Helen, maybe the engagement broken off; though he still wore the broad gold ring.

Once he did fall full-length between two rows of machines. He fell back and lay sprawled across the clear alley. I was some way from him and walking towards him when it happened and, though I started running, the first person to reach him was Lord Sweatrag. He came swiftly from behind a machine, bucket in hand and without hesitation emptied a stream of oozing black sump muck over Jock's face and neck and chest. Everyone who had been moving froze in sheer astonishment. Jock instantly revived, spluttering and raising himself into a sitting position. He knew what had happened and who had done it but it took him a few moments of violent coughing before he regained his breath, then, with the thick oil still running down his

169

face he shouted, 'Ya evil loony cunt! I'll flatten you. Whit did ye dae that for?'

'To save you the bother I've had,' said Lord Sweatrag calmly. Whatever that meant, Jock seemed to know. His angry stare flickered. The labourer added, 'Try not to spread that stuff in the alley.'

The patient was incredulous. 'Ye mean I've tae let it soak intae ma boiler suit?'

'If you can,' said Lord Sweatrag. He turned smartly about and marched away swinging the empty bucket.

Several people made tentative gestures indicating their intention of helping Jock to his feet. As he was now completely covered in wet filth they delayed just long enough to let him prove he didn't need any help. He was standing upright, like a huge black candle which was rapidly melting, when the foreman arrived. Jock shouted, 'I want that mad bastard sacked. Today!'

There was a general murmur of agreement and I saw the foreman note it. They all liked Jock and they did not like the autocratic labourer. He had a way of making many of them feel uncomfortable, even without pouring sump oil over them. The foreman himself had often been at a severe disadvantage in dealing with Lord Sweatrag, who had detailed knowledge of the whole administration of the Engine Works and of the very few inalienable rights of a labourer. He nodded reassuringly to Jock. 'Get cleaned up and then come and see me in the box.'

When Jock had gone, a bemused group remained around the spot where the black footprints started. The certainty was growing that Sweatrag would have to go or it would be a Union matter. I said, 'Maybe he was trying to help.'

'Help?'

'To bring Jock round when he fainted.'

'Wi' sump oil?'

'But it did revive him.'

'Don't be daft. Suffocation! If he was unconscious it could've killed him.'

'That's true,' I said. They took it as an admission of my stupidity but I was thinking of that odd moment of complicity between Jock and the labourer.

The foreman's box became the focus of attention for the rest of the morning and the foreman's powers were acutely weighed in various discussion groups, the members of which were ostensibly consulting each other about work. Each carried a token piece of machinery or a machine-drawing to be flourished occasionally. And the news spread. Eager emissaries from other shops arrived, work token in hand, to be briefed on what might be the first flash in a full-scale labourer revolt. Others went in search of Sweatrag and came back to report that he was still sweeping and saying nothing. Attention turned to what would happen now. Best opinion was that whereas a foreman could certainly sack one of his own men on the spot, sacking a labourer – who was technically part of a general utility, like running water – was more than a 'soft-hat' could do. That would require a 'bowler'. And sure enough, before Jock had finished cleaning up, a manager wearing his bowler hat arrived at the box. The charge-hand opened the door for him; and did not fully close it. A few minutes later, he was called in. He came out again immediately and walked straight towards me.

'Billy, you saw what happened, didn't ye?'

'Yes.'

'Ye've tae tell the boss what ye saw. Come on.'

The charge-hand and I walked like priest and acolyte through a discreetly avid congregation. It made me blush to feel all those eyes following every step I took. The manager had pushed his bowler well back on his head as he lay sprawled in the foreman's little swivel chair. The foreman stood and so did I. There were no introductions.

'Well? What happened?' asked the Bowler.

'Jock was walking towards me when he fainted. Mr Dalziel . . .'

'Who's that?'

'Sweatrag,' said the Soft-Hat.'

'Is he a Dalziel?'

'Seems so.'

'Bloody clown,' said the Bowler impartially and nodded to me to continue.

'Mr Dalziel tried to revive him.'

The Bowler smacked his lips disapprovingly and grimaced. 'You mean he tried to drown him in sump shit.'

'Perhaps he thought it was water. Mr Dalziel always has a bucket of clean water when he's doing sumps – to prime the pump when he's finished the job.'

The Bowler glanced questioningly at the Soft-Hat. He shrugged to indicate that this was a possibility then turned to me as to a hostile witness. 'That's what Sweatrag told you, I suppose?'

'No. I haven't spoken to Mr Dalziel at all about this.'

'Was there any argument between Jock and this labourer?' the Bowler wanted to know. 'Just before it happened. Any struggle? You say Jock fainted.'

'Oh, yes! He often faints.'

'Often! Then what the hell's he doin' at work?' demanded the exasperated manager of his subordinate.

The foreman glared at me. 'That's all, Billy, thank you.'

As I left the box, Jock was waiting to go in. 'Did ye tell them whit happened?'

'I told them what might have happened.'

Jock patted my shoulder, misinterpreting my contribution. 'Aye, right enough, he might have suffocated me.'

For the watching eyes I took out my Works ticket and headed in the direction of the lavatories. They would readily believe that the honour and excitement of being questioned by a manager would bring on the craps. But instead I went in search of Lord Sweatrag. I did not have to search far. He was exactly where he should have been and fastidiously continuing with his work.

'Mr Dalziel!'

He gave a tight little smile at this rare use of his name but did not immediately look up. 'Yes?'

'I've been talking to the manager about you and Jock . . .' He went on sweeping with measured strokes. 'They asked me because I saw what happened.'

'Yes?'

'And I told them you probably picked up the wrong bucket. I mean, that you intended to pick up the bucket of clean water.'

He straightened his back and leaned on the brush. No.

He rested his open palm on the top of the brush handle as though it were a magisterial staff. 'There was no mistake,' he said. 'I know which bucket is which and exactly where they are placed about me.'

'But you don't have to tell them that.'

'I don't have to tell them anything,' replied Lord Sweatrag, looking at me with weary condescension. 'Was there something you wanted me to do for you?'

'No. I came to tell you that. To give you an excuse.'

'Excuse! What makes you think that *I* would want an excuse?'

'Well – they may sack you.'

'They can do that whenever they want – with or without an excuse.'

'But if you had a good reason . . .'

'I have a good reason.'

I waited but, apparently, the audience was over and he resumed sweeping. I should have learned then that there was no point in trying to help Lord Sweatrag. He took complete responsibility for himself, however perverse his actions. Back in the shops there was a lull filled with conjecture while we waited for the accused to be brought up. It was just before lunch when he was summoned to the box to be sacked. We all knew he would be because after *his* interview Jock had told us that the manager had more or less promised to rid him of this turbulent labourer. Jock had also been told of my hypothesis, which he took as a kind of betrayal.

Sweatrag strolled to the box with maddening composure. He bore himself so upright that he seemed to be leaning backwards. Just before he stepped inside he paused and surveyed it, as though doubting the safety of such a flimsy structure; but he went in, anyway. Then we gasped as the foreman came out, presumably at Sweatrag's request. Our boss was far from pleased at this temporary eviction from his power-base and immediately engaged the hovering charge-hand in conversation about a job – as though *that* was what he'd come out for. The manager and Sweatrag were alone together for quite a while before, to everyone's surprise, Jock was recalled. 'I'm no' gonnae accept any bloody apology, I'll tell ye that,' he told us as he went. There were murmurs of approval. Nobody wanted the climax to be spoiled with an apology from the ridiculous loony. The foreman, under guise of ushering Jock in, went in again himself. We waited. However, the climax was spoiled by the horn blowing for lunch. The fascination of box-watching had distracted most of the men from their usual preparations and they cursed at having to wash their hands in their own time. And they kept glancing back as they headed for the canteen.

I decided to wait and see what happened, mainly because I was sure that Lord Sweatrag would never offer an apology. My pal, Frank, was unsettled by my failure to obey the call of the canteen.

'Come on! Don't be daft. Ye'll miss yer dinner!'

'I'll have it tomorrow.'

'Mair than likely. But ye've paid for it th'day as well.'

'I want to see their faces when they come out.'

'They'll still hiv the same faces *efter* ye've had yer dinner. Come on, Billy.'

'You go on.'

'Ye're a stubborn bugger,' he muttered as he sprinted away, overtaking the charge-hand who'd thought he was the last to leave.

Now that all the machines were off, there was a startling silence in the shop. I was reluctant to move in case the sound would be amplified and carry to the four men in the box. Gradually, I became aware of their murmuring voices, though over the distance of a hundred yards I couldn't tell which of them was speaking. That murmuring continued for twenty minutes. Then it was Jock who was first to emerge. He walked quickly to the far end of the shop where there was a water tap and a can of soluble oil. I followed him.

'What happened?'

He glanced at me with an air of suspicion or, I thought, fear. As though I knew what had happened and was trying to trap him. 'Nothing.'

'Has Mr Dalziel been sacked?'

' "*Mister* Dalziel"!' He lathered his hands with the

174

soluble oil, in lieu of soap, and began rinsing them, turning the oil magically from golden-brown to milk-white. Obviously, he did not want to discuss the matter. In silence I watched him complete the washing and the drying of his hands with a clean sweat-rag. 'Did he apologise?' I asked.

'He did not.'

'And he hasn't been sacked.'

'You seem tae know.'

'I'm just guessing.'

'Like ye were guessin' he picked up the wrang bucket.'

'What did Dalziel say?'

'Ye'd better ask him,' said Jock, and strode away in a manner which forbade any further exchange. He put on his jacket and went home.

I knew it would do no good asking Lord Sweatrag about his private conversation with the manager. And, since the foreman had been excluded from it, the normal process of information filtering from him through the charge-hand had to be excluded as well. For the rest of that week the Machine Shops were in a ferment of baffled curiosity. There was Lord Sweatrag with an air of amused superiority, and there was Jock Turnbull, muted and depressed. And Jock did not suffer any more 'blackouts' that week or in the weeks that followed. In fact he never fainted again. One might have thought he'd be grateful to Dalziel for curing him with a bucket of sump oil. Instead, he developed an obsessive hatred of the labourer, even if he had to remind himself of it from time to time – since he'd no previous experience of hating anyone. It meant remembering not to look up when Dalziel came to collect the sweat-rags and to throw them on the ground instead of handing them over. He had to remember to find Dalziel when there was any heavy material or tools to be collected from the store and to push the requisition slip into the labourer's top pocket without a word. These and many other petty actions, ritually repeated, reduced the bright-eyed, ebullient senior apprentice to an edgy bitterness. And the fact that he avoided any of his previous friendly banter with his workmates, in case they raised the subject of Lord Sweatrag, gradually isolated him. As for Lord Sweatrag, he had always been isolated – and the object of derision. He bore the efforts of an amateur hater with ease. But no secret is a secret forever, or we would not know that a secret existed. The clue came from the Drawing Office and from the 'old-wifie' of a man that Sweatrag had told me about.

Before I discovered it, though, I had to take leave of 'the tools'. Naturally my colleagues had a ceremony for that. And, inevitably, it involved genital exposure. Whereas an apprentice starting work at the tools was greased, anyone elevated to the 'staff' was washed – with a hose-pipe. You could have it stuck down the front of your trousers or you could take off all your clothes. Nor was there any consolation in the fact that they also undertook to dry the crucial area, for that was done with compressed-air nozzles. Is there any wonder, I thought, that men in the Drawing Office were said to be impotent. In my case it was remembered that, four years earlier, I'd escaped greasing. So they did the greasing first, then applied the hose-pipe, followed by the freezing jets of air. In fact the only indecent exposure I missed was the pre-nuptial rite; which is the messiest of them all. I'd seen Frank go through it and there was gleeful anticipation of Jock Turnbull.

Apart from being desperately uncomfortable, I thought the 'leaving the tools' ceremony was quite unnecessary. Going into the Drawing Office was just another aspect of the same job.

'Not at all,' said Frank. 'We're the workers, they're the staff. And *they* never let ye forget that.'

'It's still part of my apprenticeship.'

'But if ye stayed there ye'd be a Draughtsman – and that's middle-class right away.'

'Frank, I *am* middle-class.'

'Aye, *you* are. But the other fellas that go up there arenae. It's goin' through that shiny door changes them. Anyway, I'll miss ye.' To my embarrassment he took my hand and shook it. 'An' don't say A didnae look efter ye while ye were here.'

'I'm very grateful to you,' I said, trying to match my tone to that of someone embarking on a long hazardous voyage. 'Give my regards to Elsie. How is she, by the way?'

'Fine, fine. The baby's due early in May.'

'I hope everything goes well.' Then the sham solemnity overcame me and I laughed. 'Oh, this is ridiculous. I'm going to work only three hundred yards away. I'll be down to see you regularly.'

'Sure,' said Frank.

'I shall,' I promised.

'Aye, at first. But even then ye'll no' be the same.'

'Why not?'

'Because you're "staff" now, Billy, an' I'll never be "staff".'

'What's to stop you?'

'Lack o' brains,' Frank said.

I shrugged and turned away, walking up the long humming alley of machines for the last time in dirty dungarees. I passed Lord Sweatrag, busy as usual, bending over a sump. I thought he didn't see me but when I glanced back he was on his feet – almost at attention – staring wistfully after me as though at someone departing for the promised land. I reported at the Gatehouse and, with some little ceremony, gave up my 'ticket'. No longer was I No. 875; I was one of the gentlemen at boards and a man of honour who would be trusted to arrive for work in time and to leave it only with the greatest reluctance.

The following Monday I went in by a different gate and was immediately taken into custody by the man who'd got the job Lord Sweatrag wanted. As Drawing Office clerk it was his duty to note all my particulars and he seemed perfectly happy to devote a whole morning to the task. His name was Weatherby and, fortunately, he was a terrible gossip. I steered him round to the onerous nature of the position he held and wondered idly how he came to be there.

'Well, they couldnae dae wi' any roughnecks in here,' he said.

'No, of course not.' I looked down the length of the huge, hushed room and at all the heads bent over boards in waxwork concentration.

'And they want somebody they know they can trust. I mean tae say, I have access tae all the confidential records that come through this office.'

'Were there any other applicants for the job?'

He laughed – though very softly. 'Oh, aye, there were. But, of coorse, preference is given tae them that's already inside the firm.'

Not to mention inside the family, I thought – but asked, 'Did no one else in the firm apply?'

'Just Ian Dalziel,' said Weatherby. 'An' tae be honest, I thought he would have got it. I think it was his health trouble that put against him.' He agitated his jowls at the sadness of this. 'He spent eight years in an asylum, y'know – efter he came oot the Army. Then they found oot he wisnae mad at a'.'

'Really?'

'But it was his ain fault, the silly man. He worked his ticket, y'see tae get oot o' the Army and then . . .'

'Sorry?'

'Dalziel kidded on he wis mad, so that they'd gie him his discharge papers. They believed him and they discharged him. But when he got out, everybody else believed him as well and they put him away.'

'I see.' And what I was seeing was Lord Sweatrag standing, sump bucket in hand, asserting that he wanted to save Jock the trouble *he'd* had. Weatherby babbled on, then, near the end of our marathon interview, he mentioned the point which nudged the other part of the mystery into place.

The clerk referred to my written application. 'Now, ye say here that you'll be joining the Merchant Navy as soon as ye finish ye're time.'

'Yes. I have an agreement that Holts will take me.'

'Ye'd better let me have a copy o' that tae send on tae the M.O.D. or ye'll get called up straight away for yer National Service.'

'National Service.' I sighed at the sheer simplicity of the solution. It hadn't occurred to me before because I knew I wouldn't be doing National Service. But Jock Turnbull was not going to sea. He was going to get married as soon as his time was out. And, as soon as his time was out, he'd be called up to do two years in the armed forces . . . unless. Unless he failed his medical. That's what all the 'blackouts', the fainting fits had been for. He was preparing to fail his medical. He was 'working his ticket' in advance. As I sat at the empty vastness of my drawing board, perched high on my brand new stool, I wondered if it had been Jock who'd thought of the deception. No; he was too ingenuous for that – or he had been. More likely it was the idea of the redoubtable Helen. Apparently she was a young lady who always got her own way; she'd have had no intention of spending the first two years of her married life alone, on National Service pay. But if Lord Sweatrag had effectively thwarted the fainting ploy would she not think of other means? I'd been told of apprentices who pierced an ear-drum, or took small but not fatal doses of poison, or lapsed into provable sodomy in order to escape the soul-destroying boredom and bull of two years' futility. And to judge by our former colleagues who came to see us on leave, such desperate remedies were worth taking. National Service could ruin a man for life.

As I settled into my new job and concentrated on assimilating a flood of complicated information, Jock's dangers were pushed out of my mind. It was a few weeks before I came upon another nugget known to everyone in the office. Weatherby was about to retire. This was something Lord Sweatrag would have to be told at once. And in return there was something I wanted to question him upon. Perhaps there was a way in which he could help Jock and save the situation he had aborted. I couldn't very well discuss it with him in the shops where I'd now have to wear a glaring white boiler-suit as a visiting member of staff and to avoid contamination. I would go to see him at home. Old-wifie Weatherby was sure to have the address in the records. And on his own ground Lord Sweatrag would not be able to use the defence of inverted snobbery. I was determined to be firm.

'Good evening, Mr Dalziel.' He seemed much shorter wearing cardigan, corduroys and slippers. 'May I come in?'

'Mr Thompson.'

179

He opened the door wider to reveal the tidy lobby of the single-end which was on the top floor of a fairly respectable tenement in the West of the town. I felt his sharp blue eyes on me, assessing the situation, as he closed the door and gestured with the evening paper for me to precede him.

'I hope you won't think me presumptuous,' I began.

'That's no way to begin,' he said. 'Sit down. And tell me, how are you liking life in the Drawing Office?'

'It's very quiet.'

'And civilised, and clean, eh?'

'Clean, certainly.'

'And nothing heavier than paper,' he sighed and eased himself into a small chair which had never been sat in before.

'There are two things I want to talk about. First . . .'

'That's better. Always begin with the first,' he said. It was as though, in a very supercilious way, he was patting my head.

'I wanted you to know that Mr Weatherby is retiring soon.'

'Not a moment *too* soon,' Dalziel crisply observed.

'The advertisement for his replacement hasn't been published yet, so you've got time to prepare your application.'

'What application?'

It was maddening. 'Your application for his job. You're sure to get it this time.'

'But I'm not so sure that I want it, now.'

'Of course you do,' I exclaimed, and realised at once that it was the wrong attitude to take with anyone as prickly as Sweatrag. In his book – no doubt in *all* his books – wanting something was a weakness. He shifted irritably in his little unrequired chair.

'I'm not your labourer *here*, Mr Thompson,' he said.

'No, no. I meant, you *should* apply. That office needs someone with your ability. I'm afraid Weatherby has let things get into a mess. Disorder and lack of discipline. I can't think of anyone better than you to set it in order.'

He continued to glare at me then said, 'And I'm not easily taken in by flattery.'

'You must please yourself, of course.' But I knew he

would apply and I knew that, although he dare not show it, he was grateful. Gratitude was another weakness. We maintained a silence for a few moments and I noted that his 'set-in' bed was made; and made in the impenetrable fashion of beds in hospitals. It occurred to me that there must have been many aspects of the strict regimentation of a mental hospital that he relished. This stark private room could well have been the room of a private patient; with the single, uncomfortable chair for visitors who never came.

'What was the other thing?' he asked.

I gulped. If telling him good news was so difficult, how would I manage to ask him a favour? 'I'd like to talk to you about Jock Turnbull.'

'Ah!'

'I believe you spoiled his chance of avoiding National Service.'

'Do you?' His eyes widened and he smiled. It was the first time I'd seen him smile. 'Is that what you believe, Mr Thompson? And why would I do that?'

'So that he wouldn't lose his job through being unfit for work.'

'He's perfectly fit,' said Dalziel with his usual asperity.

'Yes, you knew that. And now I know that. But the manager wanted to have him signed off. Immediately.'

'There you are, then. What good would it do him evading the Army if it meant losing his job?'

'That's what I said.'

'Yes, yes.' He gave several sharp nods. 'So you did.' He smiled again – this time directly at me – evidently it was not going to be so difficult after all. 'Well, what do you want *me* to do? You've obviously got something in mind, Mr Thompson. What is it?'

'I'd like you to suggest some way in which he could still fail his medical.'

He was about to deny any knowledge of such things, but circumstances indicated that I knew better. Rather bravely he asked, 'Short of madness, you mean?'

'Preferably.'

' "Preferably",' Lord Sweatrag chuckled. It seemed he

was proud of having beaten the system, and pride was *not* a weakness. 'No, no. We can't have another loony. And he'd be no good at it anyway. He hasn't got the intelligence to be mad. He can't even faint right.'

'There must be something he *can* do.'

'I wouldn't be so sure. He's a very simple-minded young man.'

'And very likeable.'

'Is that why you are so anxious?'

'I'm afraid he'll do something stupid to please his fiancee.'

Dalziel stood up abruptly. His voice was again edged with irritation. 'In that case, you've come to the wrong person, Mr Thompson. You should go and see his fiancee.'

'I would if I thought she'd had any experience of Army medicals.'

He held his impatient pose for a few seconds, then just as abruptly sat down again. He cleared his throat. 'What I meant was, why are you taking such an interest? Surely it's none of your business.'

'It was none of yours either, but you drenched him with sump oil.'

After a long pause: 'Sump oil,' said Dalziel quietly. 'The very thing.'

'What?'

'Suppose he swallowed some of that filth? It could bring out the impetigo. There's nothing these new men detest more than an infectious skin disease. They'd mark him unfit from the other side of a glass door.'

'But he hasn't got an infectious skin disease.'

'I can't think why he hasn't. In fact it's difficult to see how a lot of them avoid it – saturating their hands in that soluble oil. That's just asking for trouble.'

'The oil doesn't affect him.'

'It would if he swallowed it,' said Dalziel. 'And now he's done that, he has a likely cause of infection. Bacteria breeding in the nose and throat transferred by the hands to the body.'

'How long would we have to wait for the symptoms?'

Dalziel looked at me pityingly. 'I'm not suggesting he

182

should really have it,' he explained. 'He has a likely cause of it, that's the main thing. The symptoms are easy to apply.'

'How?'

'A few cheap chemicals mixed into a powder he can rub on his skin. That'll give him a rash of blisters wherever he wants them. His fiancee could catch it as well, if she's keen.' He reached over and lifted a notebook from his bedside table. 'This is the mixture. Tell him to get each of these things from different chemists and then mix them in equal parts.'

'The rash wouldn't be permanent, would it?'

He shook his head. 'No. But it's got to be the right kind of blister in the right places. Any medical book will tell him where, what they should look like and what they should feel like. Impetigo – or ecthyma which sounds better. I'll make a note of that for you.'

'Why didn't you catch that, instead . . .'

'Instead of what?'

I hesitated to say it and compromised. 'Instead of doing it the hard way.'

'Huh! It was during the war and as long as you could march and point your rifle in the right direction, they didn't care if you had leprosy.'

'Surely you could march?'

'Aye. But quite often I pointed my rifle in the wrong direction – *and* pulled the trigger.'

'Did you hit anyone?'

'Only once. A fat sergeant didn't jump high enough and the bullet went right through the calf of his leg.'

'What did you dislike so much about the Army?'

'The noise. That, and being at everybody's beck and call.'

I did not say so but it seemed to me that, as a labourer in the deafening Machine Shops, Lord Sweatrag hadn't managed to escape anything.

Next day, clutching my counterfeit impetigo formula, I put on the starched white boiler-suit which hung by my peg in the Drawing Office cloakroom and went trotting down to

183

the shops in search of Jock. I'd made up my mind that I would not tell him who had devised the plan. But even then I foresaw difficulties in raising the subject. He'd have to be willing to admit the first sham to me before I could offer the better sham. As usual for him now, he was working alone, grimly rasping away with a de-ragging file. I approached him, smiling, and was about to start on my rehearsed spiel when it struck me forcibly that I might be wasting my time. The broad gold ring was missing from his finger. I waited a few moments to see if he was going to stop working, but he didn't.

'Hello, Jock.'

'Billy.' He went on filing.

'How have you been since I saw you last?'

'Fine. Just fine. A1, in fact.'

'Oh.' It was clear what that meant. I'd come too late.

'As far as the Army's concerned, anyway.'

'You've had your medical.'

'I've had it. And I've passed it.'

'That's rotten luck. When do you expect to go?'

'At the end o' next month.'

'What does Helen say?'

'Helen? Helen says it's off.'

'Your engagement!'

He nodded heavily, as though my questions were blows on his head. 'She says it's no' worth it – for her. The waitin', y'know.'

'You did all you could.'

'Aye. Gave up the chance tae go tae sea.'

'I think she's being unfair.'

'No' her fault,' Jock said. 'But I sure as Hell know who's fault it wis.'

I crackled sadly back to the office vowing that never again would I try to help anyone. I could not afford these vicarious disappointments. Another vow, which even at the time I doubted if I'd keep, was to avoid getting involved in matters that were not my business. Tony Liddle had told me something about that. I couldn't remember what it was but probably he was right.

The day after the internal notice appeared inviting applications for the post of Drawing Office Clerk, Dalziel's application was received in the office. Old Weatherby, remembering that he'd told me about the man, showed me the letter of application and I almost wept at the many pages of achingly clear copperplate writing in Indian ink, and at the care with which it had been composed. He must have started the first draft of it immediately I left him that evening. Clipped to the document was a signed chit from the department manager acknowledging that he knew of the application. The manager had to know and he would tell the foreman. If the foreman knew, the charge-hand knew. And if the charge-hand knew then everybody in the shops would know that Lord Sweatrag was attempting the impossible. I could well imagine the additional barrage of derision he would have to face that morning.

Meanwhile I did my bit in the office, telling the draughts-men how intelligent and conscientious Dalziel was and how he really shouldn't have been a labourer at all. It surprised me how willing they were to take my opinion. I mentioned this to Archie Hemple, who was the only person I knew in the place.

'I must be very convincing.'

'It's no' you,' Archie told me, 'it's your accent. Anything said in an English accent *must* be right, as far as this lot's concerned.' I laughed but he insisted. 'Naw, true enough. I'm tellin' ye, that voice is worth five years' seniority and an honours degree among these fuddy-duddies.'

To me it seemed more likely that Lord Sweatrag was called to an interview on the strength of his written application alone. He must have taken the Wednesday morning off to get dressed and ready for it because I hardly recognised the distinguished looking gentleman who went in to see the Chief. He wore a tweed hacking jacket, cavalry twill trousers and brogues. And he carried a slim but very expensive document case, probably for a sample of his notebooks. He looked like a county squire. The interview seemed to go well because the Chief came to the door with him and they were joking together. The Chief called old Weatherby over and the three of them stood chatting amiably together for some time. Oh yes, I thought, this is where Lord Sweatrag belongs.

In the afternoon I went down the shops to congratulate him on the splendid impression he'd made, and came upon disaster.

'Sweatrag's for it this time,' Frank told me. 'They caught him wi' stuff he stole fae Jock.'

'I don't believe it!'

Slowly and solemnly Frank nodded his head. 'They found the stuff in his locker, I'm tellin' ye.'

'What stuff? What stuff could he want, much less *steal* from Jock?'

'Personal belongings. Tools and gauges, they say. He could always sell them, y'know.'

'When did they find it? Who found it?'

'This mornin'.'

'While Dalziel was up in the office for his interview?'

'Seemin'ly.'

'Somebody forced open his locker and found the stuff?'

'Charge-hand says the locker wisnae locked.'

'Frank!'

'A know it sounds funny but . . . '

'It sounds ridiculous. It *is* ridiculous. And who found the stuff in the locker that wasn't locked?'

'Wan o' the other labourers. He wanted tae get the book tae check on the sweat-rags.'

For, of course, it was Wednesday and another labourer would have to take over Dalziel's usual chores. And certainly there was likely to be at least one argument about the sweat-rags to be issued. The same arguments broke out every week with labourers all over the Engine Works and were settled by whoever could shout loudest. However, the stand-in labourer in this department knew of the trouble-free way to check. There was the unassailable log book in Dalziel's locker. I marvelled at Jock Turnbull's patience and care. He had waited for his chance and had taken advantage of the ideal circumstances to get rid of the labourer he hated. And if Dalziel was sacked from the shops for theft there was no hope of his being employed in the Drawing Office. To make certain there would be no wriggling out this time Jock also insisted on having the police called.

In some desperation I cast around for a way of defeating Jock's astonishing vindictiveness. What, I wondered, if I told him that Sweatrag had given me the means for him to avoid the Army and that it was my fault it wasn't passed on in time? Would he then retract his accusation? Probably not, because then he'd still have to admit the sham 'black-outs'. And Sweatrag would have to admit his secrets, too. I was hemmed in by confidences which were the only way of explaining the sequence of events and this blatant revenge. Jock, having failed to get Sweatrag sacked from something he *did* do, was plainly elated at the prospect of getting him sacked for something he *didn't* do. He stood at his bench, happy again in a group of his former friends, as we all waited for the police to arrive. Next, I thought of going back immediately to the office and giving all my information to the Chief Draughtsman personally. But what could I prove? And even if I could prove it, the Chief – who normally would, and often did, sail against all opinion from the shops – must be chary of taking on a man who'd been questioned by the police.

First the gossip-runners brought news that Sweatrag had bolted and couldn't be found. Almost immediately the charge-hand corrected that. Sweatrag had asked for the whole day off. A policeman had gone to his home to fetch him and, no doubt, make a casual search of the premises for other stolen goods while he was there. Every quarter hour's delay increased the speculative haul which was being loaded into the police van. Then came an eye-witness report that a policeman was examining Sweatrag's locker very carefully. I paid close attention to Jock's face when that fact was relayed to his group. Surely he must have broken into the locker in order to plant the stuff. He betrayed no sign of alarm. To me that meant the he had not forced the lock but had unscrewed the back – as, on more than one occasion, I had done with my own locker when I'd lost the key. Someone was posted to keep a look-out for the police van arriving. I looked around from group to group of faces. There was a common expression and it was one of patient, expectant exultation. To my mind that small police van now moving through the streets of Greenock became a tumbril bearing a very elusive aristocrat. I said to Frank, 'All *we* need is some knitting.'

'Knittin'?'

'Round the guillotine.'

'That'll be right,' he said, not understanding and too engrossed to require an explanation.

Suddenly, *there* was Lord Sweatrag. Accompanied by a police constable he strolled down the alley that he himself kept meticulously clean. He was dressed as I had seen him in the morning and many of those watching thought at first that this was a very smart plainclothes detective with the constable in attendance. If anything, his look and bearing were more autocratic than ever and it occurred to me that he was acting the part, just a little. They went into the box where the manager already stood, guarding the recovered valuables. Jock could not wait to be summoned. Straining to keep a triumphant smile off his face he walked up to the box and went in. We prepared ourselves for another long wait while the charge was made and denied, the articles identified and examined and the labourer who 'found' them was called to give his evidence.

We were mistaken. No more than a minute elapsed before the whole sequence that we'd watched almost a year before was repeated. Again, it was Jock who came out first looking bewildered and angry. There was an audible sigh of disbelief from most of those watching. Surely the labourer hadn't got off again. Our eyes moved from the slow, weary figure of Jock to the door of the box where Lord Sweatrag emerged, head high and undeniably pleased with himself. Our attention switched back to Jock who had now reached the group at his bench. They stared at him, demanding the news which he managed to give only with great difficulty. 'He admitted it,' said Jock softly, then loud enough for all the shop to hear – 'the loony bastard admitted it!'

I felt as though a lump of joy had exploded in my chest. Spluttering at the sheer effrontery and neatness of it, I realised at once that Sweatrag had stolen – not what he was accused of – but a victory. He'd found the only way to beat

Jock and he had won. Jock knew it. His face and the tone of his voice proclaimed that he knew it. And suddenly I realised that practically everybody watching him had been aware that he'd planted the stuff in Sweatrag's locker. They shared Jock's dismay and, somehow, they too were defeated.

Lord Sweatrag, now dismissed, walked away as Mr Dalziel to collect his cards. The constable, who would then take him to the police staion, was now clearly an officer in attendance; and I was, too. I couldn't resist following in the wake of that stately exit. It was like Charles I strolling down Whitehall on his way to the block. Better, it was like *Alec Guinness* strolling down Whitehall on his way to the block, for Sweatrag was acting too. All through the shops, men came to the edge of the alleys to see him pass. He smiled occasionally and nodded. Oh yes. He was acting. He was certainly acting, but with what *style*.

Old-wifie Weatherby retired at the Fair holidays and was replaced by a man who looked even older. There was no news at all of Lord Sweatrag once he'd served his short sentence in prison. Jock Turnbull, though, made the obligatory visit to his friends down the shops and added to the horror stories of life on National Service. Frank said he was a lot thinner but looked very well in his uniform.

'Did he say anything about the theft?'

'Naw, naw. All that's over an' done wi',' said Frank. 'Jock's no' the sort o' bloke tae bear a grudge.'

'Really?'

'Anyway, he's too taken up wi' the weddin' tae think aboot anythin' else.'

'His wedding?'

'Aye. Him an' Helen. She came back tae him, seemin'ly.'

'Oh! I wonder why.'

Frank gave me a sidelong, old-fashioned look. 'Because she couldnae find such another soft-mark tae take her, I expect.'

I nodded, for that seemed likely. It also seemed inevitable that all of the effort had been wasted. Jock's effort, Dalziel's effort and – less significantly – my own, had all been made pointless through time. And the gentlemen at boards who would not notice my return – indeed, who would not notice if I never returned – did not care, either, who sat at the Clerk's desk. For I now knew that to them he was just a labourer. Maybe it was fortunate that Mr Dalziel was prevented from making that discovery.

'What are you smilin' at?' Frank asked me.

'I was just wondering if there will ever be anything I do which turns out the way I want it.'

He shook his head. 'Shouldnae think so.'

'Why not?'

'Because naebody's *got* what you want.' My long-time guide and interpreter looked closely at me to see if I understood that. And, presumably judging that I could bear it, he went on, 'What's worse, everything *you've* got is only valuable tae *you*. D'ye see whi' A mean?'

'I'm beginning to.'

He grinned. 'It's took ye a while.'

'Nearly five years.'

'Never mind, when ye qualify ye'll make a great Owner's man.'

That was less a compliment than it sounded. Everyone in the shipyard from directors to apprentices tried to steer clear of the shipowner's representative. They were civil to him, of course, and they tried to please him with bluff or excellence, but he was the enemy. He was an alien with rights and powers unfairly granted; a sort of turncoat who'd trained with the men who built ships then went over to the side of men who merely bought them.

'I'll never be an Owner's man,' I protested. But, of course, that is what I became. In a way, that's what I'd always been. No matter how devotedly I sought to become just another apprentice, and no matter how genuinely they tried to accept me, there was always the feeling that, after all, I was really a dilettante worker. And, perhaps, a dilettante human being.

TOM GALLACHER

JOURNEYMAN

'For reasons I'm ashamed of now, I was living in Montreal in the spring of 1967.'

Bill Thompson is hiding out in scruffy digs on the city's lower east side, a refugee from his own father and his father's ambitions for him. He meets Glaswegian Hugh Gillespie. From completely different backgrounds, yet they grow close. Hugh, pursuer rather than pursued, is seeking out a long vanished childhood friend.

Both sense that their lives are at a turning point. Against the blare and glare of Montreal's Expo 67 – the World Fair – optimism, idealism and wishful thinking are shown up and reduced down in the harsh light of reality.

'A perfect command of dialogue and of pace'
Norman Shrapnel in The Guardian

'Depth and complexity of viewpoint . . . I hope he will give us more'
The Scotsman

'A fast-paced novel with some of the elements of a thriller . . . It is an excellent read'
British Book News

'Very effective . . . the dialogue has always the conviction we expect of a fine playwright'
Isobel Murray in The Scotsman

Current and forthcoming titles from Sceptre

TOM GALLACHER

**JOURNEYMAN
SURVIVOR**

RONALD FRAME

SANDMOUTH PEOPLE

URSULA BENTLEY

PRIVATE ACCOUNTS

KERI HULME

THE WINDEATER

BOOKS OF DISTINCTION